William Shakespeare, William James Rolfe, William Jame Rolfe

Comedy of the two gentlemen of Verona

William Shakespeare, William James Rolfe, William Jame Rolfe

Comedy of the two gentlemen of Verona

ISBN/EAN: 9783337104160

Printed in Europe, USA, Canada, Australia, Japan

Cover: Foto ©Andreas Hilbeck / pixelio.de

More available books at **www.hansebooks.com**

SHAKESPEARE'S

COMEDY OF THE

TWO GENTLEMEN OF VERONA.

EDITED, WITH NOTES,

BY

WILLIAM J. ROLFE, LITT. D.,

FORMERLY HEAD MASTER OF THE HIGH SCHOOL, CAMBRIDGE, MASS.

WITH ENGRAVINGS.

NEW YORK:

HARPER & BROTHERS, PUBLISHERS,

FRANKLIN SQUARE.

1895.

ENGLISH CLASSICS.

EDITED BY WM. J. ROLFE, LITT. D.

Illustrated. 16mo, Cloth, 56 cents per volume; Paper, 40 cents per volume.

SHAKESPEARE'S WORKS.

The Merchant of Venice.
Othello.
Julius Cæsar.
A Midsummer-Night's Dream.
Macbeth.
Hamlet.
Much Ado about Nothing.
Romeo and Juliet.
As You Like It.
The Tempest.
Twelfth Night.
The Winter's Tale.
King John.
Richard II.
Henry IV. Part I.
Henry IV. Part II.
Henry V.
Henry VI. Part I.
Henry VI Part II.
Henry VI. Part III.

Richard III.
Henry VIII.
King Lear.
The Taming of the Shrew.
All 's Well that Ends Well.
Coriolanus.
The Comedy of Errors.
Cymbeline.
Antony and Cleopatra.
Measure for Measure.
Merry Wives of Windsor.
Love's Labour 's Lost.
Two Gentlemen of Verona.
Timon of Athens.
Troilus and Cressida.
Pericles, Prince of Tyre.
The Two Noble Kinsmen.
Venus and Adonis, Lucrece, etc.
Sonnets.
Titus Andronicus.

GOLDSMITH'S SELECT POEMS.
GRAY'S SELECT POEMS.
MINOR POEMS OF JOHN MILTON.

BROWNING'S SELECT POEMS.
BROWNING'S SELECT DRAMAS.
MACAULAY'S LAYS OF ANCIENT ROME

WORDSWORTH'S SELECT POEMS.

PUBLISHED BY HARPER & BROTHERS, NEW YORK.

The above works are for sale by all booksellers, or they will be sent by HARPER & BROTHERS to any address on receipt of price as quoted. If ordered sent by mail, 10 per cent. should be added to the price to cover cost of postage.

CONTENTS.

	PAGE
INTRODUCTION TO THE TWO GENTLEMEN OF VERONA	9
I. THE HISTORY OF THE PLAY	9
II. THE SOURCES OF THE PLOT	10
III. CRITICAL COMMENTS ON THE PLAY	11
THE TWO GENTLEMEN OF VERONA	41
ACT I	43
" II	56
" III	77
" IV	92
" V	108
NOTES	119

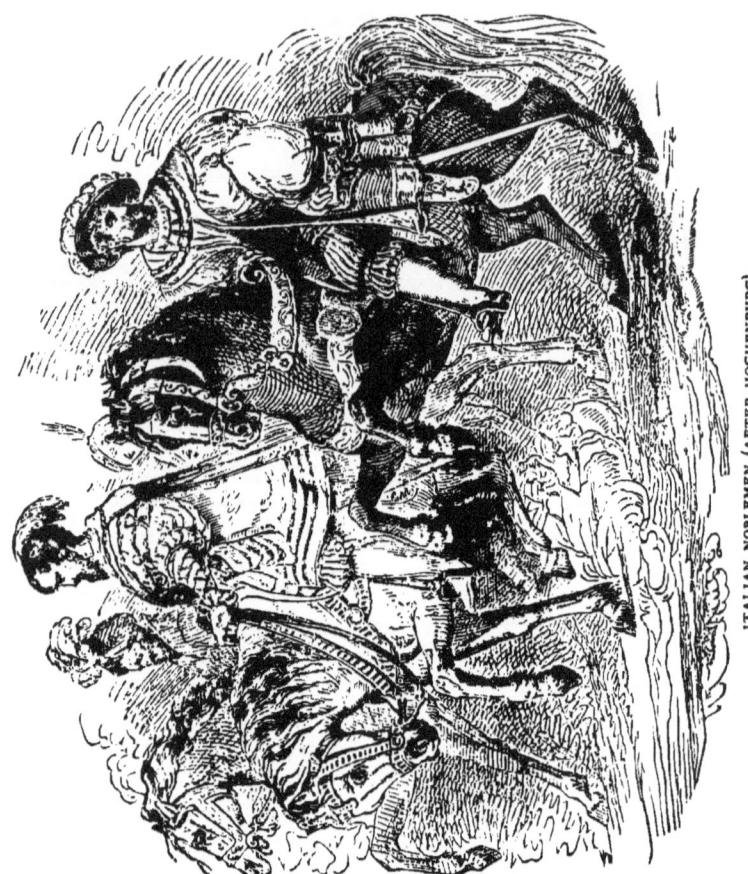

ITALIAN NOBLEMEN (AFTER HOCHENBURG).

VERONA : VIEW ON THE ADIGE.

INTRODUCTION
TO THE
TWO GENTLEMEN OF VERONA.

I. THE HISTORY OF THE PLAY.

The Two Gentlemen of Verona first appeared in the folio of 1623, where it occupies pages 20–38 in the division of "Comedies." The earliest reference to it that has been discovered

is in Meres's list of 1598 (see *C. of E.* p. 101), in which it is the
first of the six comedies mentioned. There can be no doubt
that it was one of the earliest of the plays. Malone at first
dated it in 1595, but afterwards in 1591, which cannot be far
from the truth. Collier, White, and Delius are disposed to
place it even earlier. Furnivall makes it 1591–2 (cf. *A. Y. L.*
p. 25), immediately after the *Midsummer-Night's Dream.*
Dowden is doubtful whether it preceded or followed that
play, but inclines to the former view. Fleay, in his *Manual*
(p. 28), assigns the first two acts to 1593, the rest to 1595;
in his more recent *Introduction to Shakespearian Study*
(p. 21), he dates it "circa 1595." *

The play is well printed in the folio, and the textual difficulties are comparatively few.

II. THE SOURCES OF THE PLOT.

Some of the incidents in the play are identical with those
in the *Story of the Shepherdess Felismena* in the *Diana enamo-
rada* of Jorge de Montemayor, a Portuguese poet and novel-
ist (though this romance was written in Spanish), who was
born in 1520. The *Diana* was translated by Bartholomew
Yong (or Young) as early as 1583, though his version was
not printed until 1598. The tale appears to have been dram-
atized in 1584, when a play called the *History of Felix and
Philomena* was acted at Greenwich. Shakespeare is also
supposed to have borrowed incidents or expressions from
Bandello's novel of *Apollonius and Sylla*, which was translated in 1581, and from Sidney's *Arcadia*. He was, however,
but slightly indebted to any of these sources, and some of
the coincidences that have been pointed out are probably
accidental.

* In his *Chronicle History of Shakespeare*, published in 1886, Fleay
says (p. 188): "I believe . . . that the play was produced in 1591, with
work by a second hand in it, which was cut out and replaced by Shakespeare's own in 1595." For an interesting discussion of Fleay's first
opinion, see *Trans. of New Shaks. Soc.* for 1874. p. 319 fol.

III. CRITICAL COMMENTS ON THE PLAY.

From Knight's "Pictorial Shakspere." *

"Shakspere," says Malone, "is fond of alluding to events occurring at the time when he wrote;" and Johnson observes that many passages in his works evidently show that "he often took advantage of the facts then recent, and the passions then in motion." This was a part of the *method* of Shakspere, by which he fixed the attention of his audience. The Nurse in *Romeo and Juliet* says, "It is now since the earthquake eleven years." Dame Quickly, in the *Merry Wives of Windsor*, talks of her "knights, and lords, and gentlemen, with their coaches, I warrant you, coach after coach." Coaches came into general use about 1605. "Banks's horse," which was exhibited in London in 1589, is mentioned in *Love's Labour's Lost*. These, amongst many other instances which we shall have occasion to notice, are not to be regarded as determining the period of the dramatic action; and, indeed, they are, in many cases, decided anachronisms. In the *Two Gentlemen of Verona*, there are several very curious and interesting passages which have distinct reference to the times of Elizabeth, and which, if Milan had then been under a separate ducal government, would have warranted us in placing the action of this play about half a century later than we have done. As it is, the passages are remarkable examples of Shakspere's close attention to "facts then recent;" and they show us that the spirit of enterprise, and the intellectual activity which distinguished the period when he first began to write for the stage, found a reflection in the allusions of this accurate observer. . . .

In the scene between Antonio and Panthino, where the father is recommended to "put forth" his son "to seek preferment," we have a brief but most accurate recapitulation

* Vol. i. of *Comedies*, p. 11 fol. and p. 68 fol. (by permission).

of the stirring objects that called forth the energies of the
master-spirits of the court of Elizabeth:

> "Some, to the wars, to try their fortune there;
> Some, to discover islands far away;
> Some, to the studious universities."

Here, in three lines, we have a recital of the great principles
that, either separately, or more frequently in combination,
gave their impulses to the ambition of an Essex, a Sidney, a
Raleigh, and a Drake: War, still conducted in a chivalrous
spirit, though with especial reference to the "preferment" of
the soldier; Discovery, impelled by the rapid development
of the commercial resources of the nation, and carried on in
a temper of enthusiasm which was prompted by extraordinary success and extravagant hope; and Knowledge, a thirst
for which had been excited throughout Europe by the progress of the Reformation and the invention of printing, which
opened the stores of learning freely to all men. These
pursuits had succeeded to the fierce and demoralizing passions of our long civil wars, and the more terrible conten-
tions that had accompanied the great change in the national
religion. The nation had at length what, by comparison,
was a settled government. It could scarcely be said to be
at war; for the assistance which Elizabeth afforded to the
Hugonots in France, and to those who fought for freedom of
conscience and for independence of Spanish dominion in
the Netherlands, gave a healthy stimulus to the soldiers of
fortune who drew their swords for Henry of Navarre and
Maurice of Nassau; and though the English people might
occasionally lament the fate of some brave and accomplished
leader, as they wept for the death of Sidney at Zutphen,
there was little of general suffering that might make them
look upon those wars as any thing more to be dreaded than
some well-fought tournament. Shakspere, indeed, has not
forgotten the connection between the fields where honour
and fortune were to be won by wounds, and the knightly

lists where the game of mimic war was still played upon a magnificent scale; where the courtier might, without personal danger,

> " Practise tilts and tournaments,"

before his queen, who sat in her " fortress of perfect beauty," to witness the exploits of the "foster-children of desire," amidst the sounds of cannon " fired with perfumed powder," and " moving mounts and costly chariots, and other devices."

There was another circumstance which marked the active and inquiring character of these days, which Shakspere has noticed :

> " Home-keeping youths have ever homely wits,"

exclaims Valentine, and Panthino says of Proteus, it

> " would be great impeachment to his age
> In having known no travel in his youth."

Travelling was the passion of Shakspere's times—the excitement of those who did not specially devote themselves to war, or discovery, or learning. The general practice of travelling supplies one amongst many proofs that the nation was growing commercial and rich, and that a spirit of inquiry was spread amongst the higher classes, which made it "impeachment" to their age not to have looked upon foreign lands in their season of youth and activity.

The allusions which we thus find in this comedy to the pursuits of the gallant spirits of the court of Elizabeth are very marked. The incidental notices of the general condition of the people are less decided; but a few passages that have reference to popular manners may be pointed out.

The boyhood of Shakspere was passed in a country town where the practices of the Catholic church had not been wholly eradicated either by severity or reason. We have one or two passing notices of these. Proteus, in the first scene, says,

> " I will be thy beadsman, Valentine."

Shakspere had, doubtless, seen the rosary still worn, and the
"beads bidden," perhaps even in his own house. Julia
compares the strength of her affection to the unwearied
steps of "the true-devoted pilgrim." Shakspere had, perhaps, heard the tale of some ancient denizen of a ruined abbey who had made the pilgrimage to the shrine of our Lady
of Loretto, or had even visited the sacred tomb at Jerusalem. Thurio and Proteus are to meet at "Saint Gregory's
well." This is the only instance in Shakspere in which a
holy well is mentioned; but how often must he have seen
the country people, in the early summer morning, or after
their daily labour, resorting to the fountain which had been
hallowed from the Saxon times as under the guardian influence of some venerated saint! These wells were closed and
neglected in London when Stowe wrote; but at the beginning of the last century, the custom of making journeys to
them, according to Bourne, still existed among the people of
the North; and he considers it to be "the remains of that
superstitious practice of the Papists of paying adoration to
wells and fountains." This play contains several indications of the prevailing taste for music, and exhibits an audience proficient in its technical terms; for Shakspere never
addressed words to his hearers which they could not understand. This taste was a distinguishing characteristic of the
age of Elizabeth; it was not extinct in those of the first
Charles; but it was lost amidst the puritanism of the Com-
monwealth and the profligacy of the Restoration, and has
yet to be born again amongst us. There is one allusion in
this play to the games of the people — "bid the base,"
which shows us that the social sport which the school-boy
and school-girl still enjoy—that of prison base, or prison
bars—and which still makes the village green vocal with
their mirth on some fine evening of spring, was a game of
Shakspere's days. In the long winter nights the farmer's
hearth was made cheerful by the well-known ballads of

INTRODUCTION. 15

Robin Hood; and to "Robin Hood's fat friar" Shakspere makes his Italian outlaws allude. But with music, and sports, and ales, and old wife's stories, there was still much misery in the land. "The beggar" not only spake "puling" "at Hallowmas," but his importunities or his threats were heard at all seasons. The disease of the country was vagrancy; and to this deep-rooted evil there were only applied the surface remedies to which Launce alludes, "the stocks" and "the pillory." The whole nation was still in a state of transition from semi-barbarism to civilization; but the foundations of modern society had been laid. The labourers had ceased to be vassals; the middle class had been created; the power of the aristocracy had been humbled; and the nobles had clustered round the sovereign, having cast aside the low tastes which had belonged to their fierce condition of independent chieftains. This was a state in which literature might, without degradation, be adapted to the wants of the general people; and "the best public instructor" then was the drama. Shakspere found the taste created; but it was for him, most especially, to purify and exalt it.

It is scarcely necessary, perhaps, to caution our readers against imagining that because Shakspere in this, as in all his plays, has some reference to the manners of his own country and times, he has given a false representation of the manners of the persons whom he brings upon the scene. The tone of the *Two Gentlemen of Verona* is, perhaps, not so thoroughly Italian as some of his later plays—the *Merchant of Venice*, for example; but we all along feel that his characters are not English. The allusions to home customs which we have pointed out, although curious and important as illustrations of the age of Shakspere, are so slight that they scarcely amount to any violation of the most scrupulous propriety; and regarded upon the principle which holds that in a work of art the exact should be in subordination to the higher claims of the imaginative, they are no violations of propriety at all.

*   *   *   *   *   *   *

Coleridge says, in *The Friend:* "It is Shakspere's peculiar excellence that, throughout the whole of his splendid picture gallery (the reader will excuse the acknowledged inadequacy of this metaphor), we find individuality everywhere—mere portrait nowhere. In all his various characters we still feel ourselves communing with the same nature, which is every-where present as the vegetable sap in the branches, sprays, leaves, buds, blossoms, and fruits, their shapes, tastes, and odours. Speaking of the effect, that is, his works them-selves, we may define the excellence of their method as consisting in that just proportion, that union and interpene-tration of the universal and the particular, which must ever pervade all works of decided genius and true science." Nothing can be more just and more happy than this defini-tion of the distinctive quality of Shakspere's works—a quality which puts them so immeasurably above all other works— "the union and interpenetration of the universal and the particular." It constitutes the peculiar charm of his matured style—it furnishes the key to the surpassing excellence of his representations, whether of facts which are cognizable by the understanding or by the senses, in which a single word individualizes the "particular" object described or alluded to, and, without separating it from the "universal," to which it belongs, gives it all the value of a vivid colour in a pict-ure, perfectly distinct, but also completely harmonious. The skill which he attained in this wonderful mastery over the whole world of materials for poetical construction was the re-sult of continued experiment. In his characters, especially, we see the gradual growth of this extraordinary power, as clearly as we perceive the differences between his early and his matured forms of expression. But it is evident to us, that, in his very earliest delineations of character, he had conceived the principle which was to be developed in "his splendid picture gallery." In the comedy before us, Valentine and Proteus are the "two gentlemen," Julia and Silvia the two ladies "beloved," Speed and Launce the two "clownish" servants. And yet how different is the one from the other of the same class! The German critic Gervinus has honoured us by treating "the two gentlemen," the "two ladies beloved," and the two "clownish servants," on the same principle of contrast. Proteus, who is first represented to us as a lover, is evidently a very cold and calculating one. He is "a votary to fond desire;" but he *complains* of his mistress that she has metamorphosed him :

> " Made me neglect my studies—lose my time."

He ventures, however, to write to Julia ; and when he has her answer, " her oath for love, her honour's pawn," he immediately takes the most prudent view of their position :

> "O that our fathers would applaud our loves!"

But he has not decision enough to demand this approbation :

> " I fear'd to show my father Julia's letter,
> Lest he should take exceptions to my love."

He parts with his mistress in a very formal and well-behaved style ; they exchange rings, but Julia has first offered "this remembrance" for her sake; he makes a commonplace vow of constancy, whilst Julia rushes away in tears ; he quits Verona for Milan, and has a new love at first sight the instant he sees Silvia. The mode in which he sets about betraying his friend, and wooing his new mistress, is eminently characteristic of the calculating selfishness of his nature :

> . "If I can check my erring love, I will ;
> If not, to compass her I 'll use my skill."

He is of that very numerous class of men who would always be virtuous, if virtue would accomplish their object as well as vice ; who prefer truth to lying, when lying is unneces-

B

sary; and who have a law of justice in their own minds,
which if they can observe they "will," but "if not"—if
they find themselves poor erring mortals, which they infalli-
bly do—they think

> "Their stars are more in fault than they."

This Proteus is a very contemptible fellow, who finally exhibits himself as a ruffian and a coward, and is punished by
the heaviest infliction that the generous Valentine could bestow—his forgiveness. Generous, indeed, and most confiding, is our Valentine—a perfect contrast to Proteus. In the
first scene he laughs at the passion of Proteus, as if he knew
that it was alien to his nature; but when he has become
enamoured himself, with what enthusiasm he proclaims his
devotion :

> "Why, man, she is mine own ;
> And I as rich in having such a jewel
> As twenty seas, if all their sand were pearl."

In this passionate admiration we have the germ of Romeo,
and so also in the scene where Valentine is banished :

> "And why not death, rather than living torment?"

But here is only a sketch of the strength of a deep and all-
absorbing passion. The whole speech of Valentine upon his
banishment is forcible and elegant; but compare him with
Romeo in the same condition :

> "Heaven is here
> Where Juliet lives ; and every cat, and dog,
> And little mouse, every unworthy thing,
> Live here in heaven, and may look on her,
> But Romeo may not."

We are not wandering from our purpose of contrasting Proteus and Valentine, by showing that the character of Valentine is compounded of some of the elements that we find in
Romeo; for the strong impulses of both these lovers are as

much opposed as it is possible to the subtle devices of Proteus. The confiding Valentine goes to his banishment with the cold comfort that Proteus gives him :

> "Hope is a lover's staff; walk hence with that."

He is compelled to join the outlaws, but he makes conditions with them that exhibit the goodness of his nature; and we hear no more of him till the catastrophe, when his traitorous friend is forgiven with the same confiding generosity that has governed all his intercourse with him. We have little doubt of the corruption, or, at any rate, of the unfinished nature, of the passage in which he is made to give up Silvia to his false friend—for that would be entirely inconsistent with the ardent character of his love, and an act of injustice towards Julia, which he could not commit. But it is perfectly natural and probable that he should receive Proteus again into his confidence, upon his declaration of "hearty sorrow," and that he should do so upon principle:

> "Who by repentance is not satisfied
> Is nor of heaven nor earth."

It is, to our minds, quite delightful to find in this, which we consider amongst the earliest of Shakspere's plays, that exhibition of the real Christian spirit of charity which, more or less, pervades all his writings; but which, more than any other quality, has made some persons, who deem their own morality as of a higher and purer order, cry out against them, as giving encouragement to evil-doers. We shall have occasion hereafter to speak of the noble lessons which Shakspere teaches *dramatically* (and not according to the childish devices of those who would make the dramatist write a "*moral*" at the end of five acts, upon the approved plan of a Fable in a spelling-book), and we therefore pass over, for the present, those profound critics who say "he has no moral purpose in view." But there are some who are not quite so pedantically wise as to affirm "he paid no attention to that retributive justice which, when human affairs are rightly understood, pervades them all ;" but who yet think that Proteus ought to have been at least banished, or sent to the galleys for a few years with the outlaws; that Angelo, in *Measure for Measure*, should have been hanged ; that Leontes, in the *Winter's Tale*, was not sufficiently punished for his cruel jealousy by sixteen years of sorrow and repentance; that Iachimo, in *Cymbeline*, is not treated with poetical justice when Posthumus says :

> "Kneel not to me :
> The power that I have on you is to spare you ;"—

and that Prospero is a very weak magician not to apply his power to a better purpose than only to give his wicked brother and his followers a little passing punishment—weak, indeed, when he has them in his hands, to exclaim :

> "Though with their high wrongs I am struck to the quick,
> Yet with my nobler reason 'gainst my fury
> Do I take part. The rarer action is
> In virtue than in vengeance : they being penitent,
> The sole drift of my purpose doth extend
> Not a frown further. Go release them, Ariel."

Not so thought Shakspere. He, that never represented crime as virtue, had the largest pity for the criminal. " He has never varnished over wild and blood-thirsty passions with a pleasing exterior—never clothed crime and want of principle with a false show of greatness of soul ;" but, on the other hand, he has never made the criminal a monster, and led us to flatter ourselves that he is not a man. It is as a man, subject to the same infirmities as all are who are born of woman, that he represents Proteus, and Iachimo, and other of the lesser criminals, as receiving pardon upon repentance. It is not so much that they are deserving of pardon, but that it would be inconsistent with the characters of the pardoners that they should exercise their power with severity. Shakspere lived in an age when the vindictive passions

were too frequently let loose by men of all sects and opinions, and much too frequently in the name of that religion
which came to teach peace and good-will. Is it to be objected to him, then, that wherever he could he asserted the
supremacy of charity and mercy; that he taught men the
"quality" of that blessed principle which

"Droppeth as the gentle rain from heaven;"

that he proclaimed—no doubt to the annoyance of all self-
worshippers—that "the web of our life is of a mingled yarn,
good and ill together;" and that he asked of those who
would be hard upon the wretched, "Use every man after his
desert, and who shall scape whipping?" We may be permitted to believe that this large toleration had its influence
in an age of racks and gibbets; and we know not how much
of this charitable spirit may have come to the aid of the
more authoritative and holier teaching of the same principle
—forgotten even by the teachers, but gradually finding its
way into the heart of the multitude—till human punishments
at length were compelled to be subservient to other influences
than those of the angry passions, and the laws could only
dare to ask for justice, but not for vengeance.

The generous, confiding, courageous, and forgiving spirit
of Valentine is well appreciated by the Duke—"Thou art
a gentleman." In this praise are included all the virtues
which Shakspere desired to represent in the character of
Valentine; the absence of which virtues he has also indicated in the selfish Proteus. The Duke adds, "and well derived." "Thou art a gentleman" in "thy spirit"—a gentleman in "thy unrivalled merit;" and thou hast the honours
of ancestry—the further advantage of honourable progeni-
tors. This line, in one of Shakspere's earliest plays, is a key
to some of his personal feelings. He was himself a true
gentleman, though the child of humble parents. His exquisite delineations of the female character establish the

surpassing refinement and purity of his mind in relation to
women ; and thus, if there were no other evidence of the son
of the wool-stapler of Stratford being a "gentleman," this
one prime feature of the character would be his most pre-
eminently. Well then might he, looking to himself, assert
the principle that rank and ancestry are additions to the
character of the gentleman, but not indispensable compo-
nent parts. "Thou art a gentleman, and well derived."

[From Verplanck's "Shakespeare." *]

Meres, in his list of the dramatic productions by which
Shakespeare had, before the year 1598, established the general reputation of being "the most excellent among the English in both tragedy and comedy," places the *Two Gentlemen
of Verona* first in order of thirteen dramas which he names.
. . . His poem of *Venus and Adonis*, first printed in 1592, he
himself has (in his dedication) designated as "the first heir
of his invention," and it may probably have been written before he removed to London,—and before, or not long after,
his twentieth year. The *Two Gentlemen of Verona*, if not
his earliest comedy, was in all probability written in the
same, or at least the next, stage of his intellectual progress.

Hanmer, and after him Upton, thought its style so little
resembling his general dramatic manner, that they pronounced with great confidence that "he could have had no
other hand in it than enlivening, with some speeches and
lines, thrown in here and there," the production of some inferior dramatist, from whose thoughts his own are easily to
be distinguished, "as being of a different stamp from the
rest." There seems no reasonable ground for such an
opinion ; which has, indeed, been fully refuted by Johnson,
and rejected by all succeeding critics. On the contrary,
the play is full of undeniable marks of the author, in its

* *The Illustrated Shakespeare*, edited by G. C. Verplanck (New York,
1847), vol. i. p. 5 of *T. G. of V.*

strong resemblance in taste and style to his earlier plays and poems, as well as in the indications it gives of his future power of original humour and vivid delineation of character. It, indeed, has the characteristics of a young author who had already acquired a ready and familiar mastery of poetic diction and varied versification, and who had studied nature with a poet's eye; for the play abounds in brief passages of great beauty and melody. There are here, too, as in his other early dramas, outlines of thought and touches of character, sometimes faintly or imperfectly sketched, to which he afterwards returned in his maturer years, and wrought them out into his most striking scenes and impressive passages. Thus, Julia and Silvia are, both of them, evidently early studies of female love and loveliness, from the unpractised "prentice hand" of the same great artist, who was afterwards to portray with matchless delicacy and truth the deeper affections, the nobler intellects, and the varied imaginative genius of Viola, of Rosalind, and of Imogen. Indeed, as a drama of character, however inferior to his own after-creations, it is, when compared with the works of his predecessors and contemporaries, superior alike in taste and in originality; for (as Mr. Hallam justly observes) "it was, probably, the first English comedy in which characters are drawn ideal and yet true:" although, when contrasted with the vivid and discriminating delineations to which his genius afterwards familiarized his audience, both the truth of nature and the ideal grace appear marked with the faint colouring and uncertain drawing of a timid hand. The composition, as a whole, does not seem to have been poured forth with the rapid abundance of his later works; but, in its graver parts, bears evidence of the young author's careful elaboration, seldom daring to deviate from the habits of versification to which his muse had been accustomed, and fearful of venturing on any untried novelty of expression.

Johnson (probably on the authority of his friend, Sir J. Reynolds) has well replied to the objection raised by Upton to Shakespeare's right of authorship to this piece, founded on the difference of style and manner from his other plays, by comparing this difference to the variation of manner between Raphael's first pictures and those of his ripened talent. This comparison is more apt and pregnant than Johnson's limited acquaintance with the arts of design allowed him to perceive. Raphael, as compared with other great masters of his art, was eminently the dramatic painter—the delineator of human action, passion, character, and expression; and, as the peculiar powers of his genius developed themselves by exercise, so, too, he gradually formed to himself his own taste and style of execution and expression; while, like his great dramatic antetype, his earlier works, full of grace and mind, yet bore the marks of the feebler school in which he had studied, as well as of the timidity and constraint of half-formed talent.

Not only is the language of this piece carefully studied, but there seems no haste or carelessness in the construction of the plot, unless we may admit the criticism of Judge Blackstone, whose legally trained acuteness has done for Shakespeare almost as much as the clearness and gracefulness of a style acquired in the best school of English literature has contributed to methodizing and elucidating the mysteries of his country's law. He remarks that the great fault of the play is " the hastening too abruptly, and without preparation, to the denouement, which shows that it was one of Shakespeare's very early performances." This, however, appears to be rather the want of dramatic skill, to be acquired by experience, than any effect of negligence or haste, and is, after all, no very serious fault. If, as a poem, it has little of that exuberance of thought which afterwards overflowed his page, yet, in the construction of his story, there is not only no deficiency of invention, but even more labour in that way than he was afterwards accustomed to bestow. The characters were not only new and uncopied from any dramatic model, but the plot and incidents are substantially equally original ; for, although Skottowe, and the other diligent searchers for the original materials of his dramas, have found two or three resembling incidents in Sidney's " Arcadia," and elsewhere, still there is nothing to show that the young dramatist had employed any prior story as the groundwork of his plot; and the incidents he used were such as form part of the common stock of romantic narrative.

In the humorous parts of the play, he is still more unfettered by authority, and more whimsically and boldly original. He happened to find the stage mainly abandoned in its comic underplots and interludes to the coarse buffoonery of barren-witted clowns, who excited the laughter of their audiences by jokes as coarse and practical as may be now witnessed in a modern circus. From the coarse farce of *Gammer Gurton's Needle* to Launce and Speed was a gigantic stride, even with reference to the probability of the scene ; although fastidious criticism may still find ample cause for objection. But it is now too late to protest against the improbability or the coarseness of Launce and his dog Crab. They have both of them become real and living persons of the great world of fictitious reality, and must continue to amuse generation after generation, along with Sancho and Dapple, Clinker and Chowder, and many other squires and dogs of high and low degree, whom " posterity will not willingly let die."

Upon the whole, the *Two Gentlemen of Verona*, whatever rank of merit may be assigned to it by critics, will always be read and studied with deeper interest than it can probably excite as a mere literary performance, because it exhibits to us the great dramatist at a most interesting point in his career; giving striking, but imperfect and irregular, indications of his future powers.

[*From* Charles Cowden-Clarke's "*Shakespeare-Characters.*" *]

Much interesting speculation has been bestowed upon the supposed chronology of Shakespeare's plays; and in some instances the theories appear to be highly plausible—the one of Coleridge especially so ; and this was to be expected from so acute a judge of intellectual development as well as of the structure and internal mechanism of language. More than one commentator has conjectured that the *Twelfth Night*, if not the last, was unquestionably one of the latest of our poet's compositions;† and when we take into consideration the wonderful outpouring and racy quality both of the wit and humour in that play, the exquisite polish of the diction, the richness, and, at the same time, the chastity of the poetical imagery, also the felicitous propriety and coherency of all the characters, we must perforce come to the conclusion, in comparing it with other comedies of the poet, that it was written in the full vigour and adulthood of his intellectual conformation. For the converse of this very reason, there is little doubt that the *Two Gentlemen of Verona* may be classed among the earliest of his compositions. The story (taken from a novel) is of that romantic cast and commonplace material which would attract a young writer. Item, young men falling in love ; their

> "spring of love 'resembling'
> The uncertain glory of an April day,
> Which now shows all the beauty of the sun,
> And by and by a cloud takes all away !"

One youth being faithful, the other false ; the damsels both eloping, and in disguise ; item, a pantaloon lover, rich, and

---

* From the *unpublished* "Second Series" of the *Shakespeare-Characters* (cf. 2 *Hen. IV.* p. 18), through the kindness of Mrs. Mary Cowden-Clarke.

† This was before the discovery of Manningham's diary (see *T. N.* p. 10), which showed that the play was written before 1602.—*Ed.*

therefore, of course, favoured by the father ; item, generous and very "jolly green" robbers, who, in their first interview, proclaim themselves assassins and common stabbers, and in three seconds are seized with such a spasm of admiration of the banished lover who has fallen among them that they constitute him their captain on the spot,—very like the schoolboys' game at "Watchmen and Thieves;" item, two waggish serving-men, and a chattering lady's maid—comprise the plot and its agents. It is true, that of such material is concocted a large proportion of dramatic love-scenes ; but in his *working out* the several characters in this play, even the unpractised judge will recognize a want of the poet's usual caution, as well as of artistical forethought and preparation in their development and *working up*. The changes in the events, and, above all, the impulses and actions of the individuals, are brought about with an abruptness, and an indifference to coherency, even probability, that bespeak the young practitioner.

The make-believe fierceness of the outlaws, just alluded to, is a trifle among the incongruities of character in the piece. But there is the principal agent, Proteus ; a man who "suns himself" in the esteem and confidence of all his acquaintance, is the early and bosom-friend of Valentine, is trusted (and to all appearance deservedly so) by his mistress, Julia. He leaves her with the sincerest vows of constancy ; and the moment he beholds the mistress of his friend, he not only becomes enamoured of her, but, with a wantonness of treachery, turns low, scoundrel informer to her father of their projected elopement. This not being enough to fill the measure of his villany, at the instance of that father he actually consents to become the calumniator of his unoffending friend to his friend's mistress, and afterwards to woo her for the pantaloon lover, Thurio ; an office which he nevertheless endeavours to convert to his own advantage. He next sends his own mistress's love-pledge, and by herself (disguised, however, as his page) to her rival; and, immediately after, attempts the greatest crime that man can perpetrate towards woman—against that same woman, too, whom he has vainly endeavoured to seduce from his friend; and when, in the sequel, he reads his repentance in *four* lines, he is at once accepted in *two* lines by the man he had so injured—who, with unique and amusing simplicity, says: "Then I am paid, and once again I do receive thee honest." But, to crown all, his mistress, Julia, congratulates herself upon having redeemed such a lover! All these confound-ings of the probabilities of event may be excused in a story of high romance; but where there is any profession of hu-man passion, we must look to have some regard to the con-comitant mystery of human nature in the abstract. Now, Proteus is, confessedly, a solid scoundrel; and, what is worse, he is a *mean* scoundrel. If there be any quality that a woman esteems in man, it is the high assertion of a bold, defying nature; and what most revolts her in man is a sneaking and compromising one. And this accords with the law of their physical conformation; for being formed weaker than man, as regards tendons and muscles, they look to him as their champion and defender: hence a woman enter-tains an instinctive disgust at a rascal. She will cling to a ruffian, a highwayman, even a murderer—for the higher crimes are not always unattended by generous impulses—but she will despise and shun a pettifogging sneaksby. While a man would laugh at and amuse himself with the beast, a woman would be more serious. She sees no fun in a das-tardly traitor; nor is there: there can be no hope of re-demption in a "mean" soul. In one, therefore, of Proteus's composition it is a violence offered to nature that a woman like Julia (who has witnessed the whole course of his despi-cable career) should be supposed capable to receive and wel-come him: nevertheless, she does; his repentance coming only when his plots are discovered, and the sincerity of it suspicious.

Julia herself is a perfect chrysolite of sweetness, constancy, high-mindedness, and maidenly delicacy. Of her cold-hearted and faithless lover she says : " Because I *love* him I must pity him ;" and, with the generosity of true greatness, she describes her rival, Silvia, as "a virtuous gentlewoman, mild, and beautiful." Her well-known speech to her waiting-woman, upon assuming male attire, that she may follow her lover, is equal in elegance to any thing of its class that ever was penned. Lucetta, her maid, dissuading her from her purposed elopement, Julia replies :

> "The more thou damm'st it up, the more it burns.
> The current that with gentle murmur glides,
> Thou know'st, being stopp'd, impatiently doth rage ;
> But when his fair course is not hindered,
> He makes sweet music with the enamell'd stones,
> Giving a gentle kiss to every sedge
> He overtaketh in his pilgrimage,
> And so by many winding nooks he strays
> With willing sport to the wild ocean.
> Then let me go, and hinder not my course.
> I 'll be as patient as a gentle stream,
> And make a pastime of each weary step,
> Till the last step have brought me to my love ;
> And there I 'll rest, as after much turmoil
> A blessed soul doth in Elysium."

And her last speech, when discovered as his page, is the only one bordering upon a reproach that she makes to him : this is what is meant by calling her " high-minded." She says :

> " Behold her that gave aim to all thy oaths,
> And entertain'd 'em deeply in her heart.
> How oft hast thou with perjury cleft the root !
> O Proteus, let this habit make thee blush !
> Be thou asham'd that I have took upon me
> Such an immodest raiment, if shame live
> In a disguise of love.

It is the lesser blot, modesty finds,
Women to change their shapes than men their minds."

It may possibly have been heretofore observed that the standers-by in a game always see more than the players of it ; and in nothing is this more signally exemplified than in the serious game of " Love." Shakespeare has therefore (of course) made the waiting-woman, Lucetta, with all a woman's quickness and suspicion on that point, doubt the truth and constancy of Proteus. Her conduct, when Julia has determined to follow him in male attire, is distinguished by its plain sense, and solicitude for the happiness of her mistress ; that of the mistress is all confidence and amiable blindness :

" *Julia.* Lucetta, as thou lov'st me, let me have
What thou think'st meet and is most mannerly.
But tell me, wench, how will the world repute me
For undertaking so unstaid a journey?
I fear me, it will make me scandaliz'd.
 Lucetta. If you think so, then stay at home and go not.
 Julia. Nay, that I will not.
 Lucetta. Then never dream on infamy, but go.
If Proteus like your journey when you come,
No matter who 's displeas'd when you are gone.
I fear me, he will scarce be pleas'd withal.
 Julia. That is the least, Lucetta, of my fear.
A thousand oaths, an ocean of his tears,
And instances as infinite of love,
Warrant me welcome to my Proteus.
 Lucetta. All these are servants to deceitful men.
 Julia. Base men, that use them to so base effect !
Put truer stars did govern Proteus' birth ;
His words are bonds, his oaths are oracles,
His love sincere, his thoughts immaculate,
His tears pure messengers sent from his heart,
His heart as far from fraud as heaven from earth.
 Lucetta. Pray heaven he prove so, when you come to him !
 Julia. Now, as thou lov'st me, do him not that wrong
To bear a hard opinion of his truth.
Only deserve my love by loving him ;

And presently go with me to my chamber,
To take a note of what I stand in need of,
To furnish me upon my longing journey.
All that is mine I leave at thy dispose,
My goods, my lands, my reputation ;
Only, in lieu thereof, dispatch me hence.
Come, answer not, but to it presently !
I am impatient of my tarriance."

An angelic purity and self-respect such as Julia's never could assimilate with a nature like that of Proteus. Her very quality of soul would lead her to deplore the wreck of all where she had "garner'd up her heart," and to forgive the traitor : but to unite with and love such a man were to anomalize her own creation; it were, in short, almost to demand an impossibility. In all this, however, what a glorious thing is the contemplation of our Shakespeare's gentleness of nature, and adoration of the spirit of beauty and holiness, as it shines in its calm and tranquil lustre in the loving heart of a sincere woman! In his earliest production, as in his latest—in his Julia and Silvia in the *Two Gentlemen of Verona*, and his Viola and Olivia of the *Twelfth Night*—there is the same homage to a virtuous passion ; to truth and constancy, generosity and loving-kindness. In the worthier characters among the men, too, we have in this his earliest as in his later productions the same transparent and unsuspecting nature — with magnanimity under injuries. The atonement which the Duke makes to Valentine under all his trials is of a piece with Valentine's own generous behaviour (which I fear I may have treated somewhat flippantly when alluding to the young lover's facility in forgiveness); being that of a courageous man, conscious of his own rectitude and good-will to all—even to his enemy. Posthumus dismisses the slanderer, Iachimo, in those dignified words : " Live, and deal with others better." Posthumus, however, would not have received Iachimo to his confidence : Shakespeare was a more experienced man when he wrote the *Cymbeline ;* he had learned that the thing was impossible. Yet Iachimo was not so vile a character as Proteus : nevertheless, in the same fine spirit, he makes Valentine receive the "hearty sorrow" of Proteus (his own words) as a "ransom for offence;" adding :

> "Who by repentance is not satisfied
> Is nor of heaven nor earth, for these are pleas'd."

So youthful is the constitution of this play, that I can fancy it to have been the companion of one or two others in the young poet's wallet, when he set off on his journey to London, to "seek his fortune :" and what a fortune! I repeat that it is perfectly delightful to trace this consistency of the pure Christian spirit through all the writings of our poet—our own—ours especially, and the poet of the whole earth generally. There is no vacillation in him ; he does not at one period of his career inculcate the revenge of a demon, and at another — with the questionable piety of a Maw-worm—welcome the lash of persecution. Our Shakespeare is never in extremes ; he never defies or rebels ; and he never cants : he has himself established the axiom, that "The web of our life is of a mingled yarn, good and ill together;" and no one more practically than he has inculcated the command to forgive our brother, even to the seventy-and-seventh offence. He believed that there was "good in every thing;" and he has therefore never (of his own creation) presented us with a human being of unmitigated evil : neither has he (as has been well said) "varnished over wild and blood-thirsty passions with a pleasing exterior—never clothed crime and want of principle with a false show of greatness of soul."   He has, in short, never fostered the wicked, or pandered to the Pharisee and self-worshipper: his all-abounding charity is in itself a rebuke to the "too-seeming holy," who *talk* of grace, yet shut the gates of mercy upon the weak and the frail.

Upon this subject of Shakespeare's forbearance towards the infirmities of his brother mortals, Mr. Charles Knight makes the following sound and philosophical reflection: "He lived in an age when the vindictive passions were too frequently let loose by men of all sects and opinions, and much too frequently in the name of that religion which came to teach 'peace and good-will.' Is it to be objected to him, then, that wherever he could he asserted the supremacy of charity and mercy" [and will it be believed that his very lenity towards delinquents has been made a ground of suspicion against himself?]; "that he taught men the 'quality' of that principle which 'droppeth as the gentle rain from heaven;' . . . and that he asked of those who would be hard upon the wretched, 'Use every man according to his desert, and who shall escape whipping?' We may be permitted to believe that this large toleration had its influence in an age of racks and gibbets; and we know not how much of this charitable spirit may have come to the aid of the more authoritative and holier teaching of the same principle—forgotten even by the teachers, but gradually finding its way into the heart of the multitude—till human punishments at length were compelled to be subservient to other influences than those of the angry passions, and the laws could only dare to ask for justice, but not for vengeance."

The mirth and humour in the *Two Gentlemen of Verona* are confined to the two servants, Launce and Speed. Launce, who, with his dog Crab, is as complete a piece of individuality as Sancho with his ass Dapple, is an amusing and original fellow. Some one of the commentators censures his and his brother-servant Speed's humour as being comprised of the "lowest and most trifling conceits." It had been well that some commentators had restricted themselves solely to the verifying of their text with that of the folio of 1623. "Low" the "conceits" of Messrs. Launce and Speed may be, for the authors of them are not distinguished by

C

high intellectual or social refinement; but surely the "humour" is good, of its class—quaint, rich, and uncommon—although it be not consistent with the modern tone of jesting. The "commentator" would probably have preferred the Congreve school of servants, who were quite as refined and witty as their masters. Nevertheless, Launce's upbraiding Crab with his ingratitude, and indecorous conduct in the company of other "gentlemanlike dogs" under the Duke's table, is irresistibly droll, and as droll as indecorous; and no wonder Master Launce got kicked out for fathering his minion's misbehaviour. His description, also, of his leave-taking at home, when about to accompany his master on his travels, is queer and eccentric: and it must be borne in mind that foreign travel was a grave, and, by the ignorant commonalty, thought to be a perilous adventure in those days; since, not a hundred and twenty years ago, cautious persons, when leaving Northampton for London (sixty-six miles), would make their wills; and the whole congregation of kindred, friends, and neighbours would assemble to take leave of them. So, Launce and his family are in a terrible pucker at parting:

"Nay, 't will be this hour ere I have done weeping; all the kind of the Launces have this very fault. I have received my proportion, like the prodigious son, and am going with Sir Proteus to the Imperial's court. I think Crab my dog be the sourest-natured dog that lives; my mother weeping, my father wailing, my sister crying, our maid howling, our cat wringing her hands, and all our house in a great perplexity, yet did not this cruel-hearted cur shed one tear. He is a stone, a very pebble-stone, and has no more pity in him than a dog. A Jew would have wept to have seen our parting; why, my grandam, having no eyes, look you, wept herself blind at my parting. Nay, I'll show you the manner of it. This shoe is my father;—no, this left shoe is my father;—no, no, this left shoe is my mother;—nay, that cannot be so neither;—yes, it is so, it is so, it hath the worser sole. This shoe, with the hole in it, is my mother, and this my father. A vengeance on 't! there 't is: now, sir, this staff is my sister, for, look you, she is as white as a lily and as small as a wand; this hat is Nan, our maid; I am the dog;—no, the dog is himself, and I am the dog—O, the dog is me, and I am myself; ay, so, so. Now come I to my father: Father, your blessing. Now should not the shoe speak a word for weeping: now should I kiss my father; well, he weeps on. Now come I to my mother;—O, that she·could speak now like a wood woman! Well, I kiss her; why, there 't is; here 's my mother's breath up and down. Now come I to my sister; mark the moan sne makes. Now, the dog all this while sheds not a tear nor speaks a word; but see how I lay the dust with my tears."

When his fellow-servant, Speed, eagerly inquires of him repecting his master Sir Proteus's love-suit, "But tell me true, will 't be a match?" Launce characteristically and profoundly answers: "Ask my dog: if he say ay, it will; if he say no, it will; if he shake his.tail and say nothing, it will." Launce's best spice of philosophy is where he says: "I reckon this always—that a man is never undone till he be hanged." The character of Launce reminds one in some degree, on account of its quaintness, of Launcelot Gobbo in *The Merchant of Venice:* but the humour of the former is even more eccentric—more "rum"—than that of old Shylock's serving-lad. This peculiar vein of drollery was doubtless popular in Shakespeare's day; for he has not unfrequently repeated and varied it in the characters of his men-servants.

Speed is a fellow of a "higher mark and likelihood" than Launce, who appears a sort of substitute for the "fool" in the piece; and, like the legitimate fool, a mixture of wag, zany, and monkey; and mostly monkey for trick and mischief. Speed is as lively as quicksilver; is an eternal punster; and not without cleverness in observing character. A man would own a choice round of acquaintance if Speed were his dullest companion.

As an instance of his quickness in observing character, there is not only the witty speech at the commencement of act ii., enumerating the tokens by which he knows that his master, Sir Valentine, is in love; but there is the dialogue with Sir Proteus in the first scene of the play, where Speed gives an account of his having carried a message to Julia from her lover. In this dialogue it should seem that Shakespeare meant to insinuate that Proteus, among his other defects, was a miserly fellow; for Speed, who is not his servant, but Valentine's, is obliged to push him hard in the little affair of remuneration for the trouble of dancing on his errands. It is observable, too, that when he does get the "screw to act," he only succeeds in squeezing from him one of the smallest coins. If such were really Shakespeare's design, it is but another example of his care in combining qualities to enforce and substantiate the coarser features of his characters. Penuriousness could scarcely fail to become one of the vices to compound such a nature as that of Proteus.

The play winds up with an effect of "And so, every thing ended well, and they all lived happily afterwards "—that is in delightful harmony with the simple primitiveness of the romance in the story which it dramatizes. The Duke is no less facile in his listening to reason and forgiving the lovers than the lovers have been facile in coming to a right understanding between themselves; Proteus's repentance and return to his faith towards his original mistress is no less prompt than Valentine's magnanimity of friendship; and Julia's ready belief in the future steadfastness of her hitherto fickle lover is of the same complexion with the rose-coloured hue that pervades the whole conduct of scene and personages here. There is something wonderfully youthful—almost childlike—in the tone of the close of this play, that perfectly accords with our belief in its being one of the very youngest of Shakespeare's productions; the miraculous ease of conversion from bad to good, of evil courses to righteous procedure, of inconstancy to constancy, and of narrow-mindedness to generosity, being among those miracles in which youth is prone to believe and which youthful poets delight to represent as not only possible, but natural.

[*From Mr. F. J. Furnivall's Introduction to the Play.**]

The *Two Gentlemen* is certainly far less beautiful in fancy than the *Dream*, but it is a great advance on that play in dramatic construction. Shakspere has at length settled down into that field of Italian story which is to be hereafter the scene of his greatest triumphs. As after *The Tempest*, so after the *Dream*, there seems to have been a partial exhaustion of original effort, and a falling-back on outside models. The play is strongly linked with the *Dream*. Its subject is the same, fickleness of love. Two men seek one girl; one of the men (Proteus, Demetrius) is loved by another girl (Julia, Helena), to whom he was betrothed, but whom he deserts for a time, who follows him, and whom he at last turns to again. Both couples are to be married on the same day, both girls run after their lovers, both fathers want to marry their daughters to men whom they dislike, but consent to their girls' choice at last. Hermia trusts Helena with her secret and she betrays it, Valentine trusts Proteus with his secret and Proteus betrays it. We have a Duke and a wood in both plays. The links with the *Errors* are, that Julia seeking her husband is like Adriana seeking hers. Speed and Launce are like the two Dromios; Launce and his milkmaid are like the Ephesian Dromio and his kitchenmaid, catalogue of her charms and all. We have a link with Chaucer as well as *Love's Labours Lost* in Valentine's contempt for love, and after-conquest by it, being the counterpart of Troilus as well as of Berowne. That the *Two Gentlemen* and its incidents were great favourites with Shakspere is evident from his use of them in after-plays. In *The Merchant* we have Portia's discussion of her lovers with Nerissa admirably developed from Julia's here with Lucetta, and also Portia's putting on man's dress and quizzing herself in it developed from Julia's here. This is repeated again in Rosalind in *As You Like It.*

* *The Leopold Shakspere* (London, 1877), p. xxvii. (by permission).

In *The Merchant*, too, we have Launcelot Gobbo developed from Launce, with a bit of Speed. In *Romeo and Juliet* we have Juliet going to confession like Silvia here. In *Twelfth Night* we have Viola like Julia, each as page, carrying messages of love from the man she loves to the girl he loves, to whom she tells her own story disguised ; and in each case the man whom the page-girl loves at last marries her. In *Much Ado* we have the signs of love in Benedick developed from those described by Speed here. In *All's Well* we have a parallel to the Host scene, and in *Cymbeline* we may compare Imogen with Julia. In these early plays, we have love's power over men's oaths to one another in *Love's Labours Lost*, over men's friendship and their vows to women in the *Dream* and the *Two Gentlemen*, yet in the latter friendship overcomes love in Valentine's offer to give up Silvia to Proteus. The fickleness of love is also seen in the *Errors*, the *Dream*, and the *Two Gentlemen*, as in Romeo's change from Rosalind to Juliet. Though the *Two Gentlemen* is dramatically an advance on the *Dream*, and though we have nothing undignified on the ladies' part to set against Hermia's scratching threat and Helena's long legs (except Julia's statement that if Silvia had not been kind to her she'd have scratched the eyes out of Silvia's picture), yet the drama has to an Englishman the terrible blot of Valentine's romantic friendship inducing him to offer to give up Silvia to Proteus, after the latter's threat of violating Silvia, just because Proteus says he repents. This, though possibly Italian and romantic,* offends us now, and it undoubtedly points to Shakspere's early time, as his making both his heroines run after their lovers also does. The heroine of the play is without doubt Julia : she suffers most, she loves most, she says the best things. The hero, Valentine, is a most generous, frank fellow, yet

---

* But it is certainly consistent with Shakspere's offer to give up his mistress to his friend Will, in Sonnet 40 :

"Take all my loves, my love, yea, take them all," etc.

dull withal. • He cannot understand Silvia's love-message to
him when she gives him back his own letter, and Speed has
to explain it to him. He walks into the trap the Duke has
laid for him without a grain of suspicion. But the beautiful
unselfishness of his reproach to Proteus on his base treachery, "I am sorry I must never trust thee more," his shifting
the blame to "time most accurst," show that he had somewhat of the nature of Theseus in the *Dream;* while the development in him of that serious, earnest love which we saw
in Antipholus of Syracuse for Luciana prepares us for the full
outburst of it in *Romeo and Juliet.* The lines in which Valentine laments his banishment from his love are the first
stroke of the death-knell of "banished" which rings through
the later play. There seems a contradiction in Silvia's character in her giving Proteus her picture. It looks like a yield-
ing to coquetry; but as Julia does n't feel it to be so, we can
hardly complain. That Silvia says no word to Valentine
when he rescues her, when she recovers him, must be put
down to the same fault as the slurred reunion of Ægeon and
his wife in the *Errors* — Shakspere's dramatic youth — he
must have been now 28—though the genuineness of this last
scene in the *Two Gentlemen* has been doubted by many critics, as well from its incidents as from its containing many
words used only in the *Henry the Sixth* plays. Note the
quick Italian turn for intrigue in Proteus, and in the Duke's
instant forming of the plan to entrap Valentine. Launce is
English of course, Stratford no doubt, and drawn from the
life. He seems to me a more truly original creation than
Bottom. I don't believe a Londoner could have made him.
That half-identity of doggy and horsey men with the animals
they own or tend, is to be seen still. The charming "Who
is Silvia?" makes one thankful that Shakspere's company
possessed a singer.

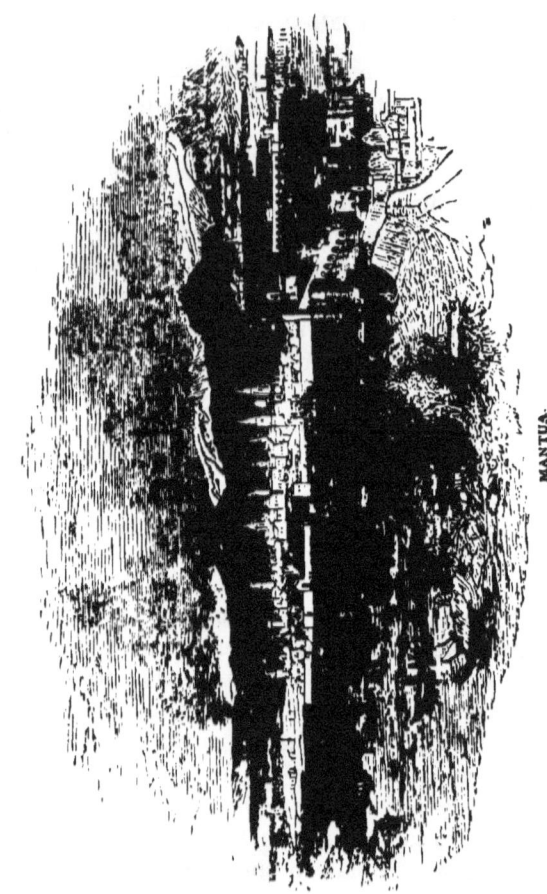

MANTUA.

TWO GENTLEMEN OF VERONA.

DRAMATIS PERSONÆ.

DUKE OF MILAN, Father to Silvia.

VALENTINE,
PROTEUS, } the two Gentlemen.

ANTONIO, Father to Proteus.

THURIO, a foolish rival to Valentine.

EGLAMOUR, Agent for Silvia in her escape.

HOST, where Julia lodges.

OUTLAWS, with Valentine.

SPEED, a clownish servant to Valentine.

LAUNCE, the like to Proteus.

PANTHINO, Servant to Antonio.

JULIA, beloved of Proteus.

SILVIA, beloved of Valentine.

LUCETTA, waiting-woman to Julia.

Servants, Musicians.

SCENE: *Verona; Milan; a forest near Milan.*

ACT I.

Scene I. *Verona. An Open Place.*

Enter VALENTINE *and* PROTEUS.

Valentine. Cease to persuade, my loving Proteus;
Home-keeping youth have ever homely wits.
Were 't not affection chains thy tender days
To the sweet glances of thy honour'd love,
I rather would entreat thy company
To see the wonders of the world abroad
Than, living dully sluggardiz'd at home,
Wear out thy youth with shapeless idleness.
But since thou lov'st, love still and thrive therein,
Even as I would when I to love begin.   10
    Proteus. Wilt thou be gone? Sweet Valentine, adieu!

Think on thy Proteus, when thou haply seest
Some rare noteworthy object in thy travel;
Wish me partaker in thy happiness
When thou dost meet good hap; and in thy danger,
If ever danger do environ thee,
Commend thy grievance to my holy prayers,
For I will be thy beadsman, Valentine.
  Valentine. And on a love-book pray for my success?
  Proteus. Upon some book I love I 'll pray for thee.   20
  Valentine. That 's on some shallow story of deep love,—
How young Leander cross'd the Hellespont.
  Proteus. That 's a deep story of a deeper love,
For he was more than over shoes in love.
  Valentine. 'T is true; for you are over boots in love,
And yet you never swum the Hellespont.
  Proteus. Over the boots? nay, give me not the boots.
  Valentine. No, I will not, for it boots thee not.
  Proteus.   What?
  Valentine. To be in love, where scorn is bought with groans,
Coy looks with heart-sore sighs, one fading moment's mirth
With twenty watchful, weary, tedious nights: 31
If haply won, perhaps a hapless gain;
If lost, why then a grievous labour won;
However, but a folly bought with wit,
Or else a wit by folly vanquished.
  Proteus. So, by your circumstance, you call me fool.
  Valentine. So, by your circumstance, I fear you 'll prove.
  Proteus. 'T is love you cavil at; I am not Love.
  Valentine. Love is your master, for he masters you;
And he that is so yoked by a fool,   40
Methinks, should not be chronicled for wise.
  Proteus. Yet writers say, as in the sweetest bud
The eating canker dwells, so eating love
Inhabits in the finest wits of all.
  Valentine. And writers say, as the most forward bud

Is eaten by the canker ere it blow,
Even so by love the young and tender wit
Is turn'd to folly, blasting in the bud,
Losing his verdure even in the prime,
And all the fair effects of future hopes.   50
But wherefore waste I time to counsel thee
That art a votary to fond desire?
Once more adieu! my father at the road
Expects my coming, there to see me shipp'd.
    Proteus. And thither will I bring thee, Valentine.
    Valentine. Sweet Proteus, no; now let us take our leave.
To Milan let me hear from thee by letters
Of thy success in love, and what news else
Betideth here in absence of thy friend;
And I likewise will visit thee with mine.   60
    Proteus. All happiness bechance to thee in Milan!
    Valentine. As much to you at home! and so, farewell.
                                                [*Exit.*

    Proteus. He after honour hunts, I after love;
He leaves his friends to dignify them more;
I leave myself, my friends and all, for love.—
Thou, Julia, thou hast metamorphos'd me,
Made me neglect my studies, lose my time,
War with good counsel, set the world at nought,
Made wit with musing weak, heart sick with thought.

Enter SPEED.

    Speed. Sir Proteus, save you! Saw you my master?   70
    Proteus. But now he parted hence, to embark for Milan.
    Speed. Twenty to one then he is shipp'd already,
And I have play'd the sheep in losing him.
    Proteus. Indeed, a sheep doth very often stray,
An if the shepherd be a while away.
    Speed. You conclude that my master is a shepherd then,
       and I a sheep?

Proteus. I do.

Speed. Why, then my horns are his horns, whether I wake or sleep.

Proteus. A silly answer, and fitting well a sheep.

Speed. This proves me still a sheep.   80

Proteus. True, and thy master a shepherd.

Speed. Nay, that I can deny by a circumstance.

Proteus. It shall go hard but I 'll prove it by another.

Speed. The shepherd seeks the sheep, and not the sheep the shepherd; but I seek my master, and my master seeks not me: therefore I am no sheep.

Proteus. The sheep for fodder follow the shepherd, the shepherd for food follows not the sheep; thou for wages followest thy master, thy master for wages follows not thee: therefore thou art a sheep.   90

Speed. Such another proof will make me cry baa.

Proteus. But, dost thou hear? gavest thou my letter to Julia?

Speed. Ay, sir; I, a lost mutton, gave your letter to her, a laced mutton, and she, a laced mutton, gave me, a lost mutton, nothing for my labour.

Proteus. Here 's too small a pasture for such store of muttons.

Speed. If the ground be overcharged, you were best stick her.   100

Proteus. Nay, in that you are astray; 't were best pound you.

Speed. Nay, sir, less than a pound shall serve me for carrying your letter.

Proteus. You mistake; I mean the pound,—a pinfold.

Speed. From a pound to a pin? fold it over and over, 'T is threefold too little for carrying a letter to your lover.

Proteus. But what said she?

Speed. [*First nodding.*] Ay.

Proteus. Nod—ay—why, that 's noddy.   110

Speed. You mistook, sir: I say, she did nod, and you ask me if she did nod; and I say ay.

Proteus. And that set together is noddy.

Speed. Now you have taken the pains to set it together, take it for your pains.

Proteus. No, no; you shall have it for bearing the letter.

Speed. Well, I perceive I must be fain to bear with you.

Proteus. Why, sir, how do you bear with me?

Speed. Marry, sir, the letter, very orderly; having nothing but the word noddy for my pains.   120

Proteus. Beshrew me, but you have a quick wit.

Speed. And yet it cannot overtake your slow purse.

Proteus. Come, come, open the matter in brief; what said she?

Speed. Open your purse, that the money and the matter may be both at once delivered.

Proteus. Well, sir, here is for your pains.   What said she?

Speed. Truly, sir, I think you 'll hardly win her.

Proteus. Why, couldst thou perceive so much from her? 129

Speed. Sir, I could perceive nothing at all from her; no, not so much as a ducat for delivering your letter: and being so hard to me that brought your mind, I fear she 'll prove as hard to you in telling your mind.   Give her no token but stones; for she 's as hard as steel.

Proteus. What, said she nothing?

Speed. No, not so much as 'Take this for thy pains.'   To testify your bounty, I thank you, you have testerned me; in requital whereof, henceforth carry your letters yourself: and so, sir, I 'll commend you to my master.   139

Proteus. Go, go, be gone, to save your ship from wrack,
Which cannot perish having thee aboard,
Being destin'd to a drier death on shore.—   [*Exit Speed.*
I must go send some better messenger;
I fear my Julia would not deign my lines,
Receiving them from such a worthless post.   [*Exit.*

Scene II.   *The Same.   Garden of Julia's House.*

Enter Julia *and* Lucetta.

Julia. But say, Lucetta, now we are alone,
Wouldst thou then counsel me to fall in love?
Lucetta. Ay, madam, so you stumble not unheedfully.
Julia. Of all the fair resort of gentlemen
That every day with parle encounter me,
In thy opinion which is worthiest love?
Lucetta. Please you repeat their names, I 'll show my mind
According to my shallow simple skill.
Julia. What think'st thou of the fair Sir Eglamour?
Lucetta. As of a knight well-spoken, neat, and fine;   10
But, were I you, he never should be mine.
Julia. What think'st thou of the rich Mercatio?
Lucetta. Well of his wealth; but of himself, so so.
Julia. What think'st thou of the gentle Proteus?
Lucetta. Lord, Lord! to see what folly reigns in us!
Julia. How now! what means this passion at his name?
Lucetta. Pardon, dear madam; 't is a passing shame
That I, unworthy body as I am,
Should censure thus on lovely gentlemen.
Julia. Why not on Proteus, as of all the rest?   20
Lucetta. Then thus,—of many good I think him best.
Julia. Your reason?
Lucetta. I have no other but a woman's reason;
I think him so because I think him so.
Julia. And wouldst thou have me cast my love on him?
Lucetta. Ay, if you thought your love not cast away.
Julia. Why he, of all the rest, hath never mov'd me.
Lucetta. Yet he, of all the rest, I think, best loves ye.
Julia. His little speaking shows his love but small.
Lucetta. Fire that 's closest kept burns most of all.   30
Julia. They do not love that do not show their love.

Lucetta. O, they love least that let men know their love.
Julia. I would I knew his mind.
Lucetta. Peruse this paper, madam.
Julia. 'To Julia.'—Say, from whom?
Lucetta. That the contents will show.
Julia. Say, say, who gave it thee?
Lucetta. Sir Valentine's page; and sent, I think, from Pro-
    teus.
He would have given it you, but I, being in the way,
Did in your name receive it; pardon the fault, I pray.   40
    Julia. Now, by my modesty, a goodly broker!
Dare you presume to harbour wanton lines?
To whisper and conspire against my youth?
Now, trust me, 't is an office of great worth,
And you an officer fit for the place.
There, take the paper; see it be return'd,
Or else return no more into my sight.
    Lucetta. To plead for love deserves more fee than hate.
    Julia. Will ye be gone?
    Lucetta.   That you may ruminate. [*Exit.*
    Julia. And yet I would I had o'erlook'd the letter.   50
It were a shame to call her back again
And pray her to a fault for which I chid her.
What fool is she, that knows I am a maid,
And would not force the letter to my view!
Since maids, in modesty, say no to that
Which they would have the profferer construe ay.
Fie, fie, how wayward is this foolish love,
That, like a testy babe, will scratch the nurse,
And presently all humbled kiss the rod!
How churlishly I chid Lucetta hence,   60
When willingly I would have had her here!
How angerly I taught my brow to frown,
When inward joy enforc'd my heart to smile!
My penance is to call Lucetta back

D

And ask remission for my folly past. —
What ho! Lucetta!

Re-enter LUCETTA.

Lucetta.   What would your ladyship?
Julia. Is 't near dinner-time?
Lucetta.   I would it were,
That you might kill your stomach on your meat,
And not upon your maid.
Julia. What is 't that you took up so gingerly?   70
Lucetta. Nothing.
Julia. Why didst thou stoop, then?
Lucetta. To take a paper up that I let fall.
Julia. And is that paper nothing?
Lucetta. Nothing concerning me.
Julia. Then let it lie for those that it concerns.
Lucetta. Madam, it will not lie where it concerns,
Unless it have a false interpreter.
Julia. Some love of yours hath writ to you in rhyme.
Lucetta. That I might sing it, madam, to a tune.   80
Give me a note; your ladyship can set.
Julia. As little by such toys as may be possible.
Best sing it to the tune of ' Light o' love.'
Lucetta. It is too heavy for so light a tune.
Julia. Heavy! belike it hath some burden then?
Lucetta. Ay, and melodious were it, would you sing it.
Julia. And why not you?
Lucetta.   I cannot reach so high.
Julia. Let 's see your song.—How now, minion!
Lucetta. Keep tune there still, so you will sing it out:
And yet methinks I do not like this tune.   90
Julia. You do not?
Lucetta.   No, madam ; it is too sharp.
Julia. You, minion, are too saucy.
Lucetta. Nay, now you are too flat,

And mar the concord with too harsh a descant;
There wanteth but a mean to fill your song.
    Julia. The mean is drown'd with your unruly base.
    Lucetta. Indeed, I bid the base for Proteus.
    Julia. This babble shall not henceforth trouble me.
Here is a coil with protestation !   [*Tears the letter.*
Go get you gone, and let the papers lie ;   100
You would be fingering them, to anger me.
    Lucetta. She makes it strange; but she would be best
        pleas'd
To be so anger'd with another letter.   [*Exit.*
    Julia. Nay, would I were so anger'd with the same!
O hateful hands, to tear such loving words !
Injurious wasps, to feed on such sweet honey,
And kill the bees that yield it with your stings !
I 'll kiss each several paper for amends.
Look, here is writ ' kind Julia.'—Unkind Julia !
As in revenge of thy ingratitude,   110
I throw thy name against the bruising stones,
Trampling contemptuously on thy disdain.
And here is writ ' love-wounded Proteus.'—
Poor wounded name ! my bosom as a bed
Shall lodge thee till thy wound be throughly heal'd;
And thus I search it with a sovereign kiss.
But twice or thrice was ' Proteus' written down.
Be calm, good wind, blow not a word away
Till I have found each letter in the letter,
Except mine own name ; that some whirlwind bear   120
Unto a ragged fearful-hanging rock,
And throw it thence into the raging sea !
Lo! here in one line is his name twice writ,
' Poor forlorn Proteus, passionate Proteus,
To the sweet Julia;' that I 'll tear away,—
And yet I will not, sith so prettily
He couples it to his complaining names.

Thus will I fold them one upon another;
Now kiss, embrace, contend, do what you will.

Re-enter LUCETTA.

Lucetta. Madam,   130
Dinner is ready, and your father stays.
Julia. Well, let us go.
Lucetta. What, shall these papers lie like tell-tales here?
Julia. If you respect them, best to take them up.
Lucetta. Nay, I was taken up for laying them down;
Yet here they shall not lie, for catching cold.
Julia. I see you have a month's mind to them.
Lucetta. Ay, madam, you may say what sights you see;
I see things too, although you judge I wink.   139
Julia. Come, come; will 't please you go?   [*Exeunt.*

SCENE III.   *The Same.   Antonio's House.*

Enter ANTONIO *and* PANTHINO.

Antonio. Tell me, Panthino, what sad talk was that
Wherewith my brother held you in the cloister?
Panthino. 'T was of his nephew Proteus, your son.
Antonio. Why, what of him?
Panthino.   He wonder'd that your lordship
Would suffer him to spend his youth at home,
While other men, of slender reputation,
Put forth their sons to seek preferment out:
Some to the wars, to try their fortune there;
Some to discover islands far away;
Some to the studious universities.   10
For any or for all these exercises
He said that Proteus your son was meet,
And did request me to importune you
To let him spend his time no more at home,
Which would be great impeachment to his age,
In having known no travel in his youth.

Antonio. Nor need'st thou much importune me to that
Whereon this month I have been hammering.
I have consider'd well his loss of time,
And how he cannot be a perfect man,   20
Not being tried and tutor'd in the world.
Experience is by industry achiev'd
And perfected by the swift course of time.
Then tell me, whither were I best to send him?
Panthino. I think your lordship is not ignorant
How his companion, youthful Valentine,
Attends the emperor in his royal court.
Antonio. I know it well.
Panthino. 'T were good, I think, your lordship sent him
   thither;
There shall he practise tilts and tournaments,   30
Hear sweet discourse, converse with noblemen,
And be in eye of every exercise
Worthy his youth and nobleness of birth.
Antonio. I like thy counsel; well hast thou advis'd:
And that thou mayst perceive how well I like it
The execution of it shall make known.
Even with the speediest expedition
I will dispatch him to the emperor's court.
Panthino. To-morrow, may it please you, Don Alphonso
With other gentlemen of good esteem   40
Are journeying to salute the emperor
And to commend their service to his will.
Antonio. Good company; with them shall Proteus go:
And—in good time!—now will we break with him.

Enter PROTEUS.

Proteus. Sweet love! sweet lines! sweet life!
Here is her hand, the agent of her heart;
Here is her oath for love, her honour's pawn.
O, that our fathers would applaud our loves,

To seal our happiness with their consents!
O heavenly Julia!   50
    Antonio. How now! what letter are you reading there?
    Proteus. May 't please your lordship, 't is a word or two
Of commendations sent from Valentine,
Deliver'd by a friend that came from him.
    Antonio. Lend me the letter; let me see what news.
    Proteus. There is no news, my lord, but that he writes
How happily he lives, how well belov'd
And daily graced by the emperor;
Wishing me with him, partner of his fortune.
    Antonio. And how stand you affected to his wish?   60
    Proteus. As one relying on your lordship's will,
And not depending on his friendly wish.
    Antonio. My will is something sorted with his wish.
Muse not that I thus suddenly proceed;
For what I will, I will, and there an end.
I am resolv'd that thou shalt spend some time
With Valentinus in the emperor's court.
What maintenance he from his friends receives,
Like exhibition thou shalt have from me.
To-morrow be in readiness to go;   70
Excuse it not, for I am peremptory.
    Proteus. My lord, I cannot be so soon provided;
Please you, deliberate a day or two.
    Antonio. Look, what thou want'st shall be sent after thee;
No more of stay! to-morrow thou must go. —
Come on, Panthino; you shall be employ'd
To hasten on his expedition.   [*Exeunt Antonio and Panthino.*
    Proteus. Thus have I shunn'd the fire for fear of burn-
        ing,
And drench'd me in the sea, where I am drown'd.
I fear'd to show my father Julia's letter,   80
Lest he should take exceptions to my love;
And with the vantage of mine own excuse

Hath he excepted most against my love.
O, how this spring of love resembleth
  The uncertain glory of an April day,
Which now shows all the beauty of the sun,
  And by and by a cloud takes all away!

Re-enter PANTHINO.

Panthino. Sir Proteus, your father calls for you.
  He is in haste; therefore, I pray you, go.
Proteus. Why, this it is: my heart accords thereto,   90
  And yet a thousand times it answers no.   [*Exeunt.*

ITALIAN GENTLEMAN (AFTER VECELLIO).

A STREET IN MILAN (SCENE V.).

ACT II.

SCENE I. *Milan. The Duke's Palace.*

Enter VALENTINE *and* SPEED.

Speed. Sir, your glove.

Valentine.   Not mine; my gloves are on.

Speed. Why, then, this may be yours, for this is but one.

Valentine. Ha! let me see; ay, give it me, it 's mine.—
Sweet ornament that decks a thing divine!
Ah, Silvia, Silvia!

Speed. Madam Silvia! Madam Silvia!

Valentine. How now, sirrah?

Speed. She is not within hearing, sir.

Valentine. Why, sir, who bade you call her?

Speed. Your worship, sir; or else I mistook.

Valentine. Well, you 'll still be too forward.

Speed. And yet I was last chidden for being too slow.

Valentine. Go to, sir; tell me, do you know Madam Silvia?

Speed. She that your worship loves?

Valentine. Why, how know you that I am in love?

Speed. Marry, by these special marks : first, you have learned, like Sir Proteus, to wreathe your arms, like a malcontent;
to relish a love-song, like a robin-redbreast; to walk alone,
like one that had the pestilence; to sigh, like a school-boy
that had lost his A B C; to weep, like a young wench that
had buried her grandam; to fast, like one that takes diet; to
watch, like one that fears robbing; to speak puling, like a
beggar at Hallowmas. You were wont, when you laughed,
to crow like a cock; when you walked, to walk like one of
the lions; when you fasted, it was presently after dinner;
when you looked sadly, it was for want of money : and now
you are metamorphosed with a mistress, that, when I look on
you, I can hardly think you my master.

Valentine. Are all these things perceived in me?

Speed. They are all perceived without ye.　　　　30

Valentine. Without me? they cannot.

Speed. Without you? nay, that 's certain, for, without you
were so simple, none else would; but you are so without
these follies, that these follies are within you and shine
through you like the water in an urinal, that not an eye that
sees you but is a physician to comment on your malady.

Valentine. But tell me, dost thou know my lady Silvia?

Speed. She that you gaze on so as she sits at supper?

Valentine. Hast thou observ'd that? even she, I mean.

Speed. Why, sir, I know her not.　　　　40

Valentine. Dost thou know her by my gazing on her, and
yet knowest her not?

Speed. Is she not hard-favoured, sir?

Valentine. Not so fair, boy, as well-favoured.

Speed. Sir, I know that well enough.

Valentine. What dost thou know?

Speed. That she is not so fair as, of you, well favoured.

Valentine. I mean that her beauty is exquisite, but her favour infinite.

Speed. That 's because the one is painted and the other out of all count.   51

Valentine. How painted? and how out of count?

Speed. Marry, sir, so painted, to make her fair, that no man counts of her beauty.

Valentine. How esteemest thou me? I account of her beauty.

Speed. You never saw her since she was deformed.

Valentine. How long hath she been deformed?

Speed. Ever since you loved her.

Valentine. I have loved her ever since I saw her, and still I see her beautiful.   61

Speed. If you love her, you cannot see her.

Valentine. Why?

Speed. Because Love is blind. O, that you had mine eyes, or your own eyes had the lights they were wont to have when you chid at Sir Proteus for going ungartered!

Valentine. What should I see then?

Speed. Your own present folly and her passing deformity; for he, being in love, could not see to garter his hose, and you, being in love, cannot see to put on your hose.   70

Valentine. Belike, boy, then, you are in love; for last morning you could not see to wipe my shoes.

Speed. True, sir, I was in love with my bed. I thank you, you swinged me for my love, which makes me the bolder to chide you for yours.

Valentine. In conclusion, I stand affected to her.

Speed. I would you were set, so your affection would cease.

Valentine. Last night she enjoined me to write some lines to one she loves.

Speed. And have you?   80

Valentine. I have.

Speed. Are they not lamely writ?

Valentine. No, boy, but as well as I can do them.—Peace! here she comes.

Speed. [*Aside*] O excellent motion! O exceeding puppet! Now will he interpret to her.

Enter SILVIA.

Valentine. Madam and mistress, a thousand good-morrows.

Speed. [*Aside*] O, give ye good even! here 's a million of manners.   89

Silvia. Sir Valentine and servant, to you two thousand.

Speed. [*Aside*] He should give her interest, and she gives it him.

Valentine. As you enjoin'd me, I have writ your letter
Unto the secret nameless friend of yours;
Which I was much unwilling to proceed in
But for my duty to your ladyship.

Silvia. I thank you, gentle servant; 't is very clerkly done.

Valentine. Now trust me, madam, it came hardly off;
For, being ignorant to whom it goes,
I writ at random, very doubtfully.   100

Silvia. Perchance you think too much of so much pains?

Valentine. No, madam; so it stead you, I will write,
Please you command, a thousand times as much;
And yet—

Silvia. A pretty period! Well, I guess the sequel;
And yet I will not name it;—and yet I care not;—
And yet take this again;—and yet I thank you,
Meaning henceforth to trouble you no more.

Speed. [*Aside*] And yet you will; and yet another yet.

Valentine. What means your ladyship? do you not like it?

Silvia. Yes, yes; the lines are very quaintly writ,   111
But since unwillingly, take them again.
Nay, take them.

Valentine. Madam, they are for you.

Silvia. Ay, ay: you writ them, sir, at my request,
But I will none of them; they are for you.
I would have had them writ more movingly.

Valentine. Please you, I 'll write your ladyship another.

Silvia. And when it 's writ, for my sake read it over,
And if it please you, so; if not, why, so.   120

Valentine. If it please me, madam, what then?

Silvia. Why, if it please you, take it for your labour.
And so, good morrow, servant.   [*Exit.*

Speed. O jest unseen, inscrutable, invisible,
As a nose on a man's face, or a weathercock on a steeple!
My master sues to her, and she hath taught her suitor,
He being her pupil, to become her tutor.
O excellent device! was there ever heard a better,
That my master, being scribe, to himself should write the
     letter?

Valentine. How now, sir? what are you reasoning with
yourself?   131

Speed. Nay, I was rhyming; 't is you that have the reason.

Valentine. To do what?

Speed. To be a spokesman for Madam Silvia.

Valentine. To whom?

Speed. To yourself: why, she wooes you by a figure.

Valentine. What figure?

Speed. By a letter, I should say.

Valentine. Why, she hath not writ to me?

Speed. What need she, when she hath made you write to
yourself? Why, do you not perceive the jest?   141

Valentine. No, believe me.

Speed. No believing you, indeed, sir. But did you perceive her earnest?

Valentine. She gave me none, except an angry word.

Speed. Why, she hath given you a letter.

Valentine.   That 's the letter I writ to her friend.

Speed. And that letter hath she deliver'd, and there an end.

Valentine. I would it were no worse.

Speed. I 'll warrant you, 't is as well: For often have you writ to her, and she, in modesty, Or else for want of idle time, could not again reply; 150 Or fearing else some messenger that might her mind discover, Herself hath taught her love himself to write unto her lover.— All this I speak in print, for in print I found it.— Why muse you, sir? 't is dinner-time.

Valentine. I have dined.

Speed. Ay, but hearken, sir; though the chameleon Love can feed on the air, I am one that am nourished by my victuals and would fain have meat. O, be not like your mistress! be moved, be moved. [*Exeunt.*

SCENE II. *Verona. Julia's House.*

Enter PROTEUS *and* JULIA.

Proteus. Have patience, gentle Julia.

Julia. I must, where is no remedy.

Proteus. When possibly I can, I will return.

Julia. If you turn not, you will return the sooner. Keep this remembrance for thy Julia's sake. [*Giving a ring.*

Proteus. Why, then, we 'll make exchange; here, take you this.

Julia. And seal the bargain with a holy kiss.

Proteus. Here is my hand for my true constancy; And when that hour o'erslips me in the day Wherein I sigh not, Julia, for thy sake, 10 The next ensuing hour some foul mischance Torment me for my love's forgetfulness! My father stays my coming; answer not; The tide is now:—nay, not thy tide of tears; That tide will stay me longer than I should.

Julia, farewell!—   [*Exit Julia.*
        What, gone without a word?
Ay, so true love should do: it cannot speak;
For truth hath better deeds than words to grace it.

Enter PANTHINO.

Panthino. Sir Proteus, you are stay'd for.
Proteus. Go; I come, I come.—   20
Alas! this parting strikes poor lovers dumb.   [*Exeunt.*

SCENE III. *The Same. A Street.*
Enter LAUNCE, *leading a dog.*

Launce. Nay, 't will be this hour ere I have done weeping;
all the kind of the Launces have this very fault. I have received my proportion, like the prodigious son, and am going
with Sir Proteus to the Imperial's court. I think Crab my
dog be the sourest-natured dog that lives; my mother weeping, my father wailing, my sister crying, our maid howling,
our cat wringing her hands, and all our house in a great perplexity, yet did not this cruel-hearted cur shed one tear. He
is a stone, a very pebble stone, and has no more pity in him
than a dog. A Jew would have wept to have seen our parting; why, my grandam, having no eyes, look you, wept herself blind at my parting. Nay, I 'll show you the manner of
it. This shoe is my father;—no, this left shoe is my father;
—no, no, this left shoe is my mother;—nay, that cannot be
so neither;—yes, it is so, it is so, it hath the worser sole.
This shoe, with the hole in it, is my mother, and this my
father. A vengeance on 't! there 't is: now, sir, this staff is
my sister, for, look you, she is as white as a lily and as small
as a wand; this hat is Nan, our maid; I am the dog;—no,
the dog is himself, and I am the dog—O! the dog is me, and
I am myself; ay, so, so. Now come I to my father: Father,
your blessing. Now should not the shoe speak a word for

weeping: now should I kiss my father; well, he weeps on. Now come I to my mother;—O, that she could speak now like an old woman! Well, I kiss her; why, there 't is; here 's my mother's breath up and down. Now come I to my sister; mark the moan she makes. Now the dog all this while sheds not a tear nor speaks a word; but see how I lay the dust with my tears.   29

Enter PANTHINO.

Panthino. Launce, away, away, aboard! thy master is shipped and thou art to post after with oars. What 's the matter? why weepest thou, man? Away, ass! you 'll lose the tide, if you tarry any longer.

Launce. It is no matter if the tied were lost; for it is the unkindest tied that ever any man tied.

Panthino. What 's the unkindest tide?

Launce. Why, he that 's tied here, Crab, my dog.

Panthino. Tut, man, I mean thou 'lt lose the flood, and, in losing the flood, lose thy voyage, and, in losing thy voyage, lose thy master, and, in losing thy master, lose thy service, and, in losing thy service,—why dost thou stop my mouth?

Launce. For fear thou shouldst lose thy tongue.   42

Panthino. Where should I lose my tongue?

Launce. In thy tale.

Panthino. In thy tail!

Launce. Lose the tide, and the voyage, and the master, and the service, and the tied! Why, man, if the river were dry, I am able to fill it with my tears; if the wind were down, I could drive the boat with my sighs.

Panthino. Come, come away, man; I was sent to call thee.

Launce. Sir, call me what thou darest.   51

Panthino. Wilt thou go?

Launce. Well, I will go.   [*Exeunt.*

SCENE IV. *Milan.   The Duke's Palace.*
Enter SILVIA, VALENTINE, THURIO, *and* SPEED.

Silvia. Servant!
Valentine. Mistress?
Speed. Master, Sir Thurio frowns on you.
Valentine. Ay, boy, it 's for love.
Speed. Not of you.
Valentine. Of my mistress, then.
Speed. 'T were good you knocked him.   [*Exit.*
Silvia. Servant, you are sad.
Valentine. Indeed, madam, I seem so.
Thurio. Seem you that you are not?   10
Valentine. Haply I do.
Thurio. So do counterfeits.
Valentine. So do you.
Thurio. What seem I that I am not?
Valentine. Wise.
Thurio. What instance of the contrary?
Valentine. Your folly.
Thurio. And how quote you my folly?
Valentine. I quote it in your jerkin.
Thurio. My jerkin is a doublet.   20
Valentine. Well, then, I 'll double your folly.
Thurio. How?
Silvia. What, angry, Sir Thurio! do you change colour?
Valentine. Give him leave, madam; he is a kind of chame-
leon.
Thurio. That hath more mind to feed on your blood than
live in your air.
Valentine. You have said, sir.
Thurio. Ay, sir, and done too, for this time.
Valentine. I know it well, sir; you always end ere you
begin.   31

Silvia. A fine volley of words, gentlemen, and quickly shot off.

Valentine. 'T is indeed, madam; we thank the giver.

Silvia. Who is that, servant?

Valentine. Yourself, sweet lady; for you gave the fire. Sir, Thurio borrows his wit from your ladyship's looks, and spends what he borrows kindly in your company.

Thurio. Sir, if you spend word for word with me, I shall make your wit bankrupt. 40

Valentine. I know it well, sir; you have an exchequer of words, and, I think, no other treasure to give your followers, for it appears, by their bare liveries, that they live by your bare words.

Silvia. No more, gentlemen, no more; here comes my father.

Enter DUKE.

Duke. Now, daughter Silvia, you are hard beset.—
Sir Valentine, your father 's in good health;
What say you to a letter from your friends
Of much good news?

Valentine. My lord, I will be thankful 50
To any happy messenger from thence.

Duke. Know ye Don Antonio, your countryman?

Valentine. Ay, my good lord, I know the gentleman
To be of worth and worthy estimation,
And not without desert so well reputed.

Duke. Hath he not a son?

Valentine. Ay, my good lord; a son that well deserves
The honour and regard of such a father.

Duke. You know him well?

Valentine. I know him as myself; for from our infancy
We have convers'd and spent our hours together: 61
And though myself have been an idle truant,
Omitting the sweet benefit of time
To clothe mine age with angel-like perfection,

E

Yet hath Sir Proteus, for that 's his name,
Made use and fair advantage of his days;
His years but young, but his experience old;
His head unmellow'd, but his judgment ripe;
And, in a word—for far behind his worth
Comes all the praises that I now bestow—   70
He is complete in feature and in mind
With all good grace to grace a gentleman.
    Duke. Beshrew me, sir, but if he make this good,
He is as worthy for an empress' love
As meet to be an emperor's counsellor.
Well, sir, this gentleman is come to me,
With commendation from great potentates,
And here he means to spend his time awhile.
I think 't is no unwelcome news to you.
    Valentine. Should I have wish'd a thing, it had been he.
    Duke. Welcome him then according to his worth.—   81
Silvia, I speak to you,—and you, sir Thurio.—
For Valentine, I need not cite him to it.
I will send him hither to you presently.   [*Exit.*
    Valentine. This is the gentleman I told your ladyship
Had come along with me, but that his mistress
Did hold his eyes lock'd in her crystal looks.
    Silvia. Belike that now she hath enfranchis'd them,
Upon some other pawn for fealty.   89
    Valentine. Nay, sure, I think she holds them prisoners still.
    Silvia. Nay, then he should be blind; and, being blind,
How could he see his way to seek out you?
    Valentine. Why, lady, Love hath twenty pair of eyes.
    Thurio. They say that Love hath not an eye at all.
    Valentine. To see such lovers, Thurio, as yourself;
Upon a homely object Love can wink.
    Silvia. Have done, have done; here comes the gentleman.
                                    [*Exit Thurio.*

Enter PROTEUS.

Valentine. Welcome, dear Proteus!—Mistress, I beseech
you,
Confirm his welcome with some special favour.
Silvia. His worth is warrant for his welcome hither,   100
If this be he you oft have wish'd to hear from.
Valentine. Mistress, it is.   Sweet lady, entertain him
To be my fellow-servant to your ladyship.
Silvia. Too low a mistress for so high a servant.
Proteus. Not so, sweet lady; but too mean a servant
To have a look of such a worthy mistress.
Valentine. Leave off discourse of disability.—
Sweet lady, entertain him for your servant.
Proteus. My duty will I boast of, nothing else.
Silvia. And duty never yet did want his meed.   110
Servant, you are welcome to a worthless mistress.
Proteus. I 'll die on him that says so but yourself.
Silvia. That you are welcome?
Proteus.   That you are worthless.

Re-enter THURIO.

Thurio. Madam, my lord your father would speak with
you.
Silvia. I wait upon his pleasure.   Come, Sir Thurio,
Go with me.—Once more, new servant, welcome.
I 'll leave you to confer of home affairs;
When you have done, we look to hear from you.
Proteus. We 'll both attend upon your ladyship.   119
                    [*Exeunt Silvia and Thurio.*
Valentine. Now, tell me, how do all from whence you came?
Proteus. Your friends are well and have them much com-
mended.
Valentine. And how do yours?
Proteus.   I left them all in health.

Valentine. How does your lady? and how thrives your
   love?
Proteus. My tales of love were wont to weary you;
I know you joy not in a love-discourse.
Valentine. Ay, Proteus, but that life is alter'd now.
I have done penance for contemning Love,
Whose high imperious thoughts have punish'd me
With bitter fasts, with penitential groans,
With nightly tears, and daily heart-sore sighs;   130
For in revenge of my contempt of love,
Love hath chas'd sleep from my enthralled eyes,
And made them watchers of mine own heart's sorrow.
O gentle Proteus, Love 's a mighty lord,
And hath so humbled me as I confess
There is no woe to his correction,
Nor to his service no such joy on earth.
Now no discourse, except it be of love;
Now can I break my fast, dine, sup, and sleep,
Upon the very naked name of love.   140
   Proteus. Enough; I read your fortune in your eye.
Was this the idol that you worship so?
   Valentine. Even she; and is she not a heavenly saint?
   Proteus. No; but she is an earthly paragon.
   Valentine. Call her divine.
   Proteus.   I will not flatter her.
   Valentine. O, flatter me; for love delights in praises.
   Proteus. When I was sick, you gave me bitter pills,
And I must minister the like to you.
   Valentine. Then speak the truth by her; if not divine,
Yet let her be a principality,   150
Sovereign to all the creatures on the earth.
   Proteus. Except my mistress.
   Valentine.   Sweet, except not any;
Except thou wilt except against my love.
   Proteus. Have I not reason to prefer mine own?

Valentine. And I will help thee to prefer her too;
She shall be dignified with this high honour,—
To bear my lady's train, lest the base earth
Should from her vesture chance to steal a kiss,
And, of so great a favour growing proud,
Disdain to root the summer-swelling flower,   160
And make rough winter everlastingly.
    Proteus. Why, Valentine, what braggardism is this?
    Valentine. Pardon me, Proteus: all I can is nothing
To her whose worth makes other worthies nothing;
She is alone.
    Proteus.   Then let her alone.
    Valentine. Not for the world! Why, man, she is mine own,
And I as rich in having such a jewel
As twenty seas, if all their sand were pearl,
The water nectar, and the rocks pure gold.
Forgive me that I do not dream on thee,   170
Because thou see'st me dote upon my love.
My foolish rival, that her father likes
Only for his possessions are so huge,
Is gone with her along, and I must after,
For love, thou know'st, is full of jealousy.
    Proteus. But she loves you?
    Valentine. Ay, and we are betroth'd: nay, more, our mar-
      riage-hour,
With all the cunning manner of our flight,
Determin'd of; how I must climb her window,
The ladder made of cords, and all the means   180
Plotted and greed on for my happiness.
Good Proteus, go with me to my chamber,
In these affairs to aid me with thy counsel.
    Proteus. Go on before; I shall inquire you forth.
I must unto the road, to disembark
Some necessaries that I needs must use,
And then I 'll presently attend you.

Valentine. Will you make haste?

Proteus. I will.—   [*Exit Valentine.*

Even as one heat another heat expels,   190
Or as one nail by strength drives out another,
So the remembrance of my former love
Is by a newer object quite forgotten.
Is it mine eye, or Valentinus' praise,
Her true perfection, or my false transgression,
That makes me reasonless to reason thus?
She is fair; and so is Julia that I love—
That I did love, for now my love is thaw'd;
Which, like a waxen image 'gainst a fire,
Bears no impression of the thing it was.   200
Methinks my zeal to Valentine is cold,
And that I love him not as I was wont.
O, but I love his lady too too much,
And that 's the reason I love him so little.
How shall I dote on her with more advice,
That thus without advice begin to love her!
'T is but her picture I have yet beheld,
And that hath dazzled my reason's light;
But when I look on her perfections,
There is no reason but I shall be blind.   210
If I can check my erring love, I will;
If not, to compass her I 'll use my skill.   [*Exit.*

Scene V. *The Same. A Street.*

Enter Speed *and* Launce *severally.*

Speed. Launce! by mine honesty, welcome to Milan!

Launce. Forswear not thyself, sweet youth, for I am not welcome. I reckon this always,—that a man is never un-done till he be hanged, nor never welcome to a place till some certain shot be paid and the hostess say welcome.

Speed. Come on, you madcap, I 'll to the alehouse with you

presently, where, for one shot of five pence, thou shalt have
five thousand welcomes. But, sirrah, how did thy master part
with Madam Julia?

Launce. Marry, after they closed in earnest, they parted
very fairly in jest.   11

Speed. But shall she marry him?

Launce. No.

Speed. How then? shall he marry her?

Launce. No, neither.

Speed. What, are they broken?

Launce. No, they are both as whole as a fish.

Speed. Why, then, how stands the matter with them?

Launce. Marry, thus; when it stands well with him, it
stands well with her.   20

Speed. What an ass art thou! I understand thee not.

Launce. What a block art thou, that thou canst not! My
staff understands me.

Speed. What thou sayest?

Launce. Ay, and what I do too: look thee, I 'll but lean,
and my staff understands me.

Speed. It stands under thee, indeed.

Launce. Why, stand-under and under-stand is all one.

Speed. But tell me true, will 't be a match?

Launce. Ask my dog: if he say ay, it will; if he say no, it
will; if he shake his tail and say nothing, it will.   31

Speed. The conclusion is then that it will.

Launce. Thou shalt never get such a secret from me but
by a parable.

Speed. 'T is well that I get it so. But, Launce, how sayest
thou, that my master is become a notable lover?

Launce. I never knew him otherwise.

Speed. Than how?

Launce. A notable lubber, as thou reportest him to be.

Speed. Why, thou whoreson ass, thou mistakest me.   40

Launee. Why, fool, I meant not thee; I meant thy master.

Speed. I tell thee, my master is become a hot lover.

Launce. Why, I tell thee, I care not though he burn him-self in love.   If thou wilt, go with me to the alehouse; if not, thou art an Hebrew, a Jew, and not worth the name of a Christian.

Speed. Why?

Launce. Because thou hast not so much charity in thee as to go to the ale with a Christian.   Wilt thou go?

Speed. At thy service.   [*Exeunt.*

SCENE VI.   *The Same.   The Duke's Palace.*

Enter PROTEUS.

Proteus. To leave my Julia, shall I be forsworn;
To love fair Silvia, shall I be forsworn;
To wrong my friend, I shall be much forsworn;
And even that power which gave me first my oath
Provokes me to this threefold perjury;
Love bade me swear, and Love bids me forswear.
O sweet-suggesting Love, if thou hast sinn'd,
Teach me, thy tempted subject, to excuse it!
At first I did adore a twinkling star,
But now I worship a celestial sun.   10
Unheedful vows may heedfully be broken,
And he wants wit that wants resolved will
To learn his wit to exchange the bad for better.
Fie, fie, unreverend tongue! to call her bad,
Whose sovereignty so oft thou hast preferr'd
With twenty thousand soul-confirming oaths.
I cannot leave to love, and yet I do;
But there I leave to love where I should love.
Julia I lose and Valentine I lose:
If I keep them, I needs must lose myself;   20
If I lose them, thus find I by their loss
For Valentine myself, for Julia Silvia.

I to myself am dearer than a friend,
For love is still most precious in itself;
And Silvia—witness Heaven, that made her fair!—
Shows Julia but a swarthy Ethiope.
I will forget that Julia is alive,
Remembering that my love to her is dead;
And Valentine I 'll hold an enemy,
Aiming at Silvia as a sweeter friend.   30
I cannot now prove constant to myself,
Without some treachery us'd to Valentine.
This night he meaneth with a corded ladder
To climb celestial Silvia's chamber-window,
Myself in counsel, his competitor.
Now presently I 'll give her father notice
Of their disguising and pretended flight,
Who, all enrag'd, will banish Valentine,
For Thurio, he intends, shall wed his daughter;
But, Valentine being gone, I 'll quickly cross   40
By some sly trick blunt Thurio's dull proceeding. –
Love, lend me wings to make my purpose swift,
As thou hast lent me wit to plot this drift!.   [*Exit.*

SCENE VII.   *Verona.   Julia's House.*
Enter JULIA *and* LUCETTA.

Julia. Counsel, Lucetta; gentle girl, assist me;
And even in kind love I do conjure thee,
Who art the table wherein all my thoughts
Are visibly character'd and engrav'd,
To lesson me, and tell me some good mean
How, with my honour, I may undertake
A journey to my loving Proteus.
Lucetta. Alas, the way is wearisome and long!
Julia. A true-devoted pilgrim is not weary
To measure kingdoms with his feeble steps;   10
Much less shall she that hath Love's wings to fly,

And when the flight is made to one so dear,
Of such divine perfection, as Sir Proteus.
   Lucetta. Better forbear till Proteus make return.
   Julia. O, know'st thou not his looks are my soul's food?
Pity the dearth that I have pined in,
By longing for that food so long a time.
Didst thou but know the inly touch of love,
Thou wouldst as soon go kindle fire with snow
As seek to quench the fire of love with words.   20
   Lucetta. I do not seek to quench your love's hot fire,
But qualify the fire's extreme rage,
Lest it should burn above the bounds of reason.
   Julia. The more thou damm'st it up, the more it burns.
The current that with gentle murmur glides,
Thou know'st, being stopp'd, impatiently doth rage :
But when his fair course is not hindered,
He makes sweet music with the enamell'd stones,
Giving a gentle kiss to every sedge
He overtaketh in his pilgrimage,   30
And so by many winding nooks he strays
With willing sport to the wild ocean.
Then let me go, and hinder not my course.
I 'll be as patient as a gentle stream,
And make a pastime of each weary step,
Till the last step have brought me to my love;
And there I 'll rest, as after much turmoil
A blessed soul doth in Elysium.
   Lucetta. But in what habit will you go along?
   Julia. Not like a woman; for I would prevent   40
The loose encounters of lascivious men.
Gentle Lucetta, fit me with such weeds
As may beseem some well-reputed page.
   Lucetta. Why, then, your ladyship must cut your hair.
   Julia. No, girl; I 'll knit it up in silken strings
With twenty odd-conceited true-love knots.

To be fantastic may become a youth
Of greater time than I shall show to be.
   Lucetta. What fashion, madam, shall I make your breeches?
   Julia. That fits as well as ' Tell me, good my lord,   50
What compass will you wear your farthingale ?'
Why even what fashion thou best lik'st, Lucetta.
   Lucetta. You must needs have them with a codpiece, madam.
   Julia. Out, out, Lucetta! that will be ill-favour'd.
   Lucetta. A round hose, madam, now 's not worth a pin,
Unless you have a codpiece to stick pins on.
   Julia. Lucetta, as thou lov'st me, let me have
What thou think'st meet and is most mannerly.
But tell me, wench, how will the world repute me
For undertaking so unstaid a journey?   ·   60
I fear me it will make me scandaliz'd.
   Lucetta. If you think so, then stay at home and go not.
   Julia. Nay, that I will not.
   Lucetta. Then never dream on infamy, but go.
If Proteus like your journey when you come,
No matter who 's displeas'd when you are gone.
I fear me, he will scarce be pleas'd withal.
   Julia. That is the least, Lucetta, of my fear.
A thousand oaths, an ocean of his tears,
And instances of infinite of love,   70
Warrant me welcome to my Proteus.
   Lucetta. All these are servants to deceitful men.
   Julia. Base men, that use them to so base effect!
But truer stars did govern Proteus' birth;
His words are bonds, his oaths are oracles,
His love sincere, his thoughts immaculate,
His tears pure messengers sent from his heart,
His heart as far from fraud as heaven from earth.
   Lucetta. Pray heaven he prove so, when you come to him!
   Julia. Now, as thou lov'st me, do him not that wrong   80
To bear a hard opinion of his truth.

Only deserve my love by loving him;
And presently go with me to my chamber,
To take a note of what I stand in need of,
To furnish me upon my longing journey.
All that is mine I leave at thy dispose,
My goods, my lands, my reputation;
Only, in lieu thereof, dispatch me hence.
Come, answer not, but to it presently!
I am impatient of my tarriance.   [*Exeunt.*

COSTUME OF PAGE (FROM PAUL VERONESE).

Such weeds
As may beseem some well-reputed page (ii. 7. 42).

MILAN.

ACT III.

Scene I. *Milan. The Duke's Palace.*

Enter Duke, Thurio, *and* Proteus.

Duke. Sir Thurio, give us leave, I pray, awhile;
We have some secrets to confer about.—   [*Exit Thurio.*
Now, tell me, Proteus, what 's your will with me?

Proteus. My gracious lord, that which I would discover
The law of friendship bids me to conceal;
But when I call to mind your gracious favours
Done to me, undeserving as I am,
My duty pricks me on to utter that
Which else no worldly good should draw from me.
Know, worthy prince, Sir Valentine, my friend,   10
This night intends to steal away your daughter;
Myself am one made privy to the plot.

I know you have determin'd to bestow her
On Thurio, whom your gentle daughter hates;
And should she thus be stolen away from you,
It would be much vexation to your age.
Thus, for my duty's sake, I rather chose
To cross my friend in his intended drift
Than, by concealing it, heap on your head
A pack of sorrows which would press you down,   20
Being unprevented, to your timeless grave.
    Duke. Proteus, I thank thee for thine honest care;
Which to requite, command me while I live.
This love of theirs myself have often seen.
Haply when they have judg'd me fast asleep,
And oftentimes have purpos'd to forbid
Sir Valentine her company and my court;
But fearing lest my jealous aim might err,
And so unworthily disgrace the man,
A rashness that I ever yet have shunn'd,   30
I gave him gentle looks, thereby to find
That which thyself hast now disclos'd to me.
And, that thou mayst perceive my fear of this,
Knowing that tender youth is soon suggested,
I nightly lodge her in an upper tower,
The key whereof myself have ever kept;
And thence she cannot be convey'd away.
    Proteus. Know, noble lord, they have devis'd a mean
How he her chamber-window will ascend,
And with a corded ladder fetch her down;   40
For which the youthful lover now is gone,
And this way comes he with it presently,
Where, if it please you, you may intercept him.
But, good my lord, do it so cunningly
That my discovery be not aimed at;
For love of you, not hate unto my friend,
Hath made me publisher of this pretence.

Duke. Upon mine honour, he shall never know
That I had any light from thee of this.   49
Proteus. Adieu, my lord; Sir Valentine is coming. [*Exit.*

Enter VALENTINE.

Duke. Sir Valentine, whither away so fast?
Valentine. Please it your grace, there is a messenger
That stays to bear my letters to my friends,
And I am going to deliver them.
Duke. Be they of much import?
Valentine. The tenour of them doth but signify
My health and happy being at your court.
Duke. Nay then, no matter; stay with me awhile.
I am to break with thee of some affairs
That touch me near, wherein thou must be secret.   60
'T is not unknown to thee that I have sought
To match my friend Sir Thurio to my daughter.
Valentine. I know it well, my Lord, and, sure, the match
Were rich and honourable; besides, the gentleman
Is full of virtue, bounty, worth, and qualities
Beseeming such a wife as your fair daughter.
Cannot your grace win her to fancy him?
Duke. No, trust me; she is peevish, sullen, froward,
Proud, disobedient, stubborn, lacking duty,
Neither regarding that she is my child   70
Nor fearing me as if I were her father:
And, may I say to thee, this pride of hers,
Upon advice, hath drawn my love from her;
And, where I thought the remnant of mine age
Should have been cherish'd by her childlike duty,
I now am full resolv'd to take a wife,
And turn her out to who will take her in.
Then let her beauty be her wedding-dower;
For me and my possessions she esteems not.
Valentine. What would your grace have me to do in this?

Duke. There is a lady of Verona here,
Whom I affect; but she is nice and coy,
And nought esteems my aged eloquence.
Now therefore would I have thee to my tutor—
For long agone I have forgot to court;
Besides, the fashion of the time is chang'd—
How and which way I may bestow myself
To be regarded in her sun-bright eye.
Valentine. Win her with gifts, if she respect not words.
Dumb jewels often in their silent kind   90
More than quick words do move a woman's mind.
Duke. But she did scorn a present that I sent her.
Valentine. A woman sometimes scorns what best contents
    her.
Send her another; never give her o'er,
For scorn at first makes after-love the more.
If she do frown, 't is not in hate of you,
But rather to beget more love in you.
If she do chide, 't is not to have you gone;
For why, the fools are mad if left alone.
Take no repulse, whatever she doth say;   100
For 'get you gone,' she doth not mean ' away!'
Flatter and praise, commend, extol their graces;
Though ne'er so black, say they have angels' faces.
That man that hath a tongue, I say, is no man,
If with his tongue he cannot win a woman.
Duke. But she I mean is promis'd by her friends
Unto a youthful gentleman of worth,
And kept severely from resort of men,
That no man hath access by day to her.
Valentine. Why, then, I would resort to her by night.   110
Duke. Ay, but the doors be lock'd and keys kept safe,
That no man hath recourse to her by night.
Valentine. What lets but one may enter at her window?
Duke. Her chamber is aloft, far from the ground,

And built so shelving that one cannot climb it
Without apparent hazard of his life.
   Valentine. Why then, a ladder quaintly made of cords,
To cast up, with a pair of anchoring hooks,
Would serve to scale another Hero's tower,
So bold Leander would adventure it.   120
   Duke. Now, as thou art a gentleman of blood,
Advise me where I may have such a ladder.
   Valentine. When would you use it? pray, sir, tell me that.
   Duke. This very night; for Love is like a child,
That longs for every thing that he can come by.
   Valentine. By seven o'clock I 'll get you such a ladder.
   Duke. But, hark thee ; I will go to her alone.
How shall I best convey the ladder thither?
   Valentine. It will be light, my lord, that you may bear it
Under a cloak that is of any length.   130
   Duke. A cloak as long as thine will serve the turn?
   Valentine. Ay, my good lord.
   Duke.   Then let me see thy cloak ;
I 'll get me one of such another length.
   Valentine. Why, any cloak will serve the turn, my lord.
   Duke. How shall I fashion me to wear a cloak?
I pray thee, let me feel thy cloak upon me.
What letter is this same? What 's here? ' *To Silvia!* '
And here an engine fit for my proceeding.
I 'll be so bold to break the seal for once.
[Reads] ' *My thoughts do harbour with my Silvia nightly,*   140
      And slaves they are to me that send them flying.
   O, could their master come and go as lightly,
      Himself would lodge where senseless they are lying!
   My herald thoughts in thy pure bosom rest them;
      While I, their king, that hither them importune,
   Do curse the grace that with such grace hath bless'd them,
      Because myself do want my servants' fortune.
   I curse myself, for they are sent by me,
                    F

That they should harbour where their lord would be.'
What 's here?   130
   ' *Silvia, this night I will enfranchise thee.'*
'T is so; and here 's the ladder for the purpose.
Why, Phaethon,—for thou art Merops' son,—
Wilt thou aspire to guide the heavenly car,
And with thy daring folly burn the world?
Wilt thou reach stars because they shine on thee?
Go, base intruder! overweening slave!
Bestow thy fawning smiles on equal mates,
And think my patience, more than thy desert,
Is privilege for thy departure hence.   163
Thank me for this more than for all the favours
Which all too much I have bestow'd on thee.
But if thou linger in my territories
Longer than swiftest expedition
Will give thee time to leave our royal court,
By heaven! my wrath shall far exceed the love
I ever bore my daughter or thyself.
Be gone! I will not hear thy vain excuse;
But, as thou lov'st thy life, make speed from hence.   [*Exit.*
 Valentine. And why not death rather than living torment?
To die is to be banish'd from myself,   171
And Silvia is myself; banish'd from her
Is self from self,—a deadly banishment!
What light is light, if Silvia be not seen?
What joy is joy, if Silvia be not by?
Unless it be to think that she is by,
And feed upon the shadow of perfection.
Except I be by Silvia in the night,
There is no music in the nightingale;
Unless I look on Silvia in the day,   180
There is no day for me to look upon;
She is my essence, and I leave to be,
If I be not by her fair influence

Foster'd, illumin'd, cherish'd, kept alive.
I fly not death, to fly this deadly doom:
Tarry I here, I but attend on death:
But, fly I hence, I fly away from life.

Enter PROTEUS *and* LAUNCE.

Proteus. Run, boy, run, run, and seek him out.
Launce. So ho, so ho!
Proteus. What seest thou?
Launce. Him we go to find; there 's not a hair on 's head
but 't is a Valentine.
Proteus. Valentine?
Valentine. No.
Proteus. Who then? his spirit?
Valentine. Neither.
Proteus. What then?
Valentine. Nothing.
Launce. Can nothing speak?—Master, shall I strike?
Proteus. Who wouldst thou strike? 200
Launce. Nothing.
Proteus. Villain, forbear.
Launce. Why, sir, I 'll strike nothing; I pray you,—
Proteus. Sirrah, I say, forbear.—Friend Valentine, a word.
Valentine. My ears are stopt and cannot hear good news,
So much of bad already hath possess'd them.
Proteus. Then in dumb silence will I bury mine,
For they are harsh, untuneable, and bad.
Valentine. Is Silvia dead?
Proteus. No, Valentine. 210
Valentine. No Valentine, indeed, for sacred Silvia.—
Hath she forsworn me?
Proteus. No, Valentine.
Valentine. No Valentine, if Silvia have forsworn me.—
What is your news?
Launce. Sir, there is a proclamation that you are vanished.

Proteus. That thou art banished—O, that 's the news!—
From hence, from Silvia, and from me thy friend.
    Valentine. O, I have fed upon this woe already,
And now excess of it will make me surfeit.   220
Doth Silvia know that I am banished?
    Proteus. Ay, ay; and she hath offer'd to the doom—
Which, unrevers'd, stands in effectual force—
A sea of melting pearl, which some call tears.
Those at her father's churlish feet she tender'd;
With them, upon her knees, her humble self;
Wringing her hands, whose whiteness so became them
As if but now they waxed pale for woe:
But neither bended knees, pure hands held up,
Sad sighs, deep groans, nor silver-shedding tears,   230
Could penetrate her uncompassionate sire;
But Valentine, if he be ta'en, must die.
Besides, her intercession chaf'd him so,
When she for thy repeal was suppliant,
That to close prison he commanded her,
With many bitter threats of biding there.
    Valentine. No more, unless the next word that thou speak'st
Have some malignant power upon my life;
If so, I pray thee, breathe it in mine ear,
As ending anthem of my endless dolour.   240
    Proteus. Cease to lament for that thou canst not help,
And study help for that which thou lament'st.
Time is the nurse and breeder of all good.
Here if thou stay, thou canst not see thy love;
Besides, thy staying will abridge thy life.
Hope is a lover's staff; walk hence with that,
And manage it against despairing thoughts.
Thy letters may be here, though thou art hence,
Which, being writ to me, shall be deliver'd
Even in the milk-white bosom of thy love.   250
The time now serves not to expostulate;

Come, I 'll convey thee through the city gate,
And, ere I part with thee, confer at large
Of all that may concern thy love-affairs.
As thou lov'st Silvia, though not for thyself,
Regard thy danger, and along with me!

Valentine. I pray thee, Launce, an if thou seest my boy,
Bid him make haste and meet me at the North-gate.

Proteus. Go, sirrah, find him out.—Come, Valentine.

Valentine. O my dear Silvia! Hapless Valentine!   260
                    [*Exit Valentine and Proteus.*

Launce. I am but a fool, look you, and yet I have the wit
to think my master is a kind of a knave; but that 's all one,
if he but one knave. He lives not now that knows me to be
in love, yet I am in love; but a team of horse shall not pluck
that from me; nor who 't is I love; and yet 't is a woman;
but what woman, I will not tell myself; and yet 't is a milkmaid; yet 't is not a maid, for she hath had gossips; yet 't is
a maid, for she is her master's maid, and serves for wages.
She hath more qualities than a water-spaniel, which is much
in a bare Christian. [*Pulling out a paper.*] Here is a cate-
log of her condition. '*Imprimis: She can fetch and carry.*'
Why, a horse can do no more: nay, a horse cannot fetch, but
only carry; therefore is she better than a jade. '*Item: She
can milk;*' look you, a sweet virtue in a maid with clean
hands.

                    Enter SPEED.

Speed. How now, Signior Launce! what news with your
mastership.

Launce. With my master's ship? why, it is at sea.

Speed. Well, your old vice still; mistake the word. What
news, then, in your paper?   280

Launce. The blackest news that ever thou heardest.

Speed. Why, man, how black?

Launce. Why, as black as ink.

Speed. Let me read them.

Launce. Fie on thee, jolt-head! thou canst not read.

Speed. Thou liest; I can.

Launce. I will try thee.   Tell me this : who begot thee?

Speed. Marry, the son of my grandfather.

Launce. O illiterate loiterer! it was the son of thy grand-
mother; this proves that thou canst not read.   290

Speed. Come, fool, come; try me in thy paper.

Launce. There; and Saint Nicholas be thy speed!

Speed. [Reads] '*Imprimis: She can milk.*'

Launce. Ay, that she can.

Speed. '*Item: She brews good ale.*'

Launce. And thereof comes the proverb, Blessing of your
heart, you brew good ale.

Speed. '*Item: She can sew.*'

Launce. That 's as much as to say, Can she so?

Speed. '*Item: She can knit.*'   300

Launce. What need a man care for a stock with a wench,
when she can knit him a stock.

Speed. '*Item: She can wash and scour.*'

Launce. A special virtue; for then she need not be wash-
ed and scoured.

Speed. '*Item: She can spin.*'

Launce. Then may I set the world on wheels, when she
can spin for her living.

Speed. '*Item: She hath many nameless virtues.*'   309

Launce. That 's as much as to say, bastard virtues, that, indeed, know not their fathers and therefore have no names.

Speed. '*Here follow her vices.*'

Launce. Close at the heels of her virtues.

Speed. '*Item: She is not to be kissed fasting, in respect of
her breath.*'

Launce. Well, that fault may be mended with a breakfast.
Read on.

Speed. '*Item: She hath a sweet mouth.*'

Launce. That makes amends for her sour breath.

Speed. '*Item: She doth talk in her sleep.*'   320

Launce. It 's no matter for that, so she sleep not in her talk.

Speed. '*Item: She is slow in words.*'

Launce. O villain, that set this down among her vices! To be slow in words is a woman's only virtue; I pray thee, out with 't, and place it for her chief virtue.

Speed. '*Item: She is proud.*'

Launce. Out with that too; it was Eve's legacy, and cannot be ta'en from her.

Speed. '*Item: She hath no teeth.*'   330

Launce. I care not for that neither, because I love crusts.

Speed. '*Item: She is curst.*'

Launce. Well, the best is, she hath no teeth to bite.

Speed. '*Item: She will often praise her liquor.*'

Launce. If her liquor be good, she shall: if she will not, I will; for good things should be praised.

Speed. '*Item: She is too liberal.*'

Launce. Of her tongue she cannot, for that 's writ down she is slow of; of her purse she shall not, for that I 'll keep shut: now, of another thing she may, and that I cannot help. Well, proceed.   341

Speed. '*Item: She hath more hair than wit, and more faults than hairs, and more wealth than faults.*'

Launce. Stop there; I 'll have her: she was mine, and not mine, twice or thrice in that last article. Rehearse that once more.

Speed. '*Item: She hath more hair than wit,*'—

Launce. More hair than wit? It may be; I 'll prove it. The cover of the salt hides the salt, and therefore it is more than the salt; the hair that covers the wit is more than the wit, for the greater hides the less. What 's next?   351

Speed. '*And more faults than hairs,*'—

Launce. That 's monstrous; O, that that were out!

Speed. '*And more wealth than faults.*'

Launce. Why, that word makes the faults gracious. Well,
I 'll have her; and if it be a match, as nothing is impossible,—

Speed. What then?

Launce. Why, then will I tell thee—that thy master stays
for thee at the North-gate.   30

Speed. For me?

Launce. For thee! ay, who art thou? he hath stayed for a
better man than thee.

Speed. And must I go to him?

Launce. Thou must run to him, for thou hast stayed so
long that going will scarce serve the turn.

Speed. Why didst not tell me sooner? pox of your love-
letters!   [*Exit.*

Launce. Now will he be swinged for reading my letter,—an
unmannerly slave, that will thrust himself into secrets! I 'll
after, to rejoice in the boy's correction.   [*Exit.*

SCENE II.   *The Same.   The Duke's Palace.*

Enter DUKE *and* THURIO.

Duke. Sir Thurio, fear not but that she will love you,
Now Valentine is banish'd from her sight.

Thurio. Since his exile she hath despis'd me most,
Forsworn my company and rail'd at me,
That I am desperate of obtaining her.

Duke. This weak impress of love is as a figure
Trenched in ice, which with an hour's heat
Dissolves to water and doth lose his form.
A little time will melt her frozen thoughts,
And worthless Valentine shall be forgot.—   10

Enter PROTEUS.

How now, Sir Proteus! Is your countryman
According to our proclamation gone?

Proteus. Gone, my good lord.

Duke. My daughter takes his going grievously.

Proteus. A little time, my lord, will kill that grief.

Duke. So I believe, but Thurio thinks not so.
Proteus, the good conceit I hold of thee—
For thou hast shown some sign of good desert—
Makes me the better to confer with thee.

Proteus. Longer than I prove loyal to your grace   20
Let me not live to look upon your grace.

Duke. Thou know'st how willingly I would effect
The match between Sir Thurio and my daughter.

Proteus. I do, my lord.

Duke. And also, I think, thou art not ignorant
How she opposes her against my will.

Proteus. She did, my lord, when Valentine was here.

Duke. Ay, and perversely she persevers so.
What might we do to make the girl forget
The love of Valentine and love Sir Thurio?   30

Proteus. The best way is to slander Valentine
With falsehood, cowardice, and poor descent,
Three things that women highly hold in hate.

Duke. Ay, but she 'll think that it is spoke in hate.

Proteus. Ay, if his enemy deliver it;
Therefore it must with circumstance be spoken
By one whom she esteemeth as his friend.

Duke. Then you must undertake to slander him.

Proteus. And that, my lord, I shall be loath to do;
'T is an ill office for a gentleman,   40
Especially against his very friend.

Duke. Where your good word cannot advantage him,
Your slander never can endamage him;
Therefore the office is indifferent,
Being entreated to it by your friend.

Proteus. You have prevail'd, my lord. If I can do it
By aught that I can speak in his dispraise,

She shall not long continue love to him.
But say this weed her love from Valentine,
It follows not that she will love Sir Thurio.   50
Thurio. Therefore, as you unwind her love from him,
Lest it should ravel and be good to none,
You must provide to bottom it on me;
Which must be done by praising me as much
As you in worth dispraise Sir Valentine.
Duke. And, Proteus, we dare trust you in this kind,
Because we know, on Valentine's report,
You are already Love's firm votary,
And cannot soon revolt and change your mind.
Upon this warrant shall you have access   60
Where you with Silvia may confer at large;
For she is lumpish, heavy, melancholy,
And, for your friend's sake, will be glad of you,
Where you may temper her by your persuasion
To hate young Valentine and love my friend.
Proteus. As much as I can do, I will effect.—
But you, Sir Thurio, are not sharp enough;
You must lay lime to tangle her desires
By wailful sonnets, whose composed rhymes
Should be full-fraught with serviceable vows.   70
Duke. Ay,
Much is the force of heaven-bred poesy.
Proteus. Say that upon the altar of her beauty
You sacrifice your tears, your sighs, your heart.
Write till your ink be dry, and with your tears
Moist it again, and frame some feeling line
That may discover such integrity;
For Orpheus' lute was strung with poets' sinews.
Whose golden touch could soften steel and stones,
Make tigers tame, and huge leviathans   80
Forsake unsounded deeps to dance on sands.
After your dire-lamenting elegies,

Visit by night your lady's chamber-window
With some sweet consort; to their instruments
Tune a deploring dump: the night's dead silence
Will well become such sweet-complaining grievance.
This, or else nothing, will inherit her.

 Duke. This discipline shows thou hast been in love.

 Thurio. And thy advice this night I 'll put in practice
Therefore, sweet Proteus, my direction-giver,   90
Let us into the city presently
To sort some gentlemen well skill'd in music.
I have a sonnet that will serve the turn
To give the onset to thy good advice.

 Duke. About it, gentlemen!

 Proteus. We 'll wait upon your grace till after supper,
And afterward determine our proceedings.

 Duke. Even now about it! I will pardon you. [*Exeunt.*

ROBIN HOOD'S FAT FRIAR (iv. 1. 36).

ACT IV.

Scene I.   *A Forest near Milan.*

Enter certain Outlaws.

1 *Outlaw.* Fellows, stand fast; I see a passenger.

2 *Outlaw.* If there be ten, shrink not, but down with 'em.

Enter Valentine *and* Speed.

3 *Outlaw.* Stand, sir, and throw us that you have about ye;
If not, we 'll make you sit and rifle you.

Speed. Sir, we are undone; these are the villains
That all the travellers do fear so much.
Valentine. My friends,—
1 *Outlaw.* That's not so, sir; we are your enemies.
2 *Outlaw.* Peace, we'll hear him.
3 *Outlaw.* Ay, by my beard, will we, for he's a proper man.
Valentine. Then know that I have little wealth to lose.   11
A man I am cross'd with adversity;
My riches are these poor habiliments,
Of which if you should here disfurnish me,
You take the sum and substance that I have.
2 *Outlaw.* Whither travel you?
Valentine. To Verona.
1 *Outlaw.* Whence came you?
Valentine. From Milan.
3 *Outlaw.* Have you long sojourned there?   20
Valentine. Some sixteen months, and longer might have
stay'd,
If crooked fortune had not thwarted me.
1 *Outlaw.* What, were you banish'd thence?
Valentine. I was.
2 *Outlaw.* For what offence?
Valentine. For that which now torments me to rehearse.
I kill'd a man, whose death I much repent;
But yet I slew him manfully in fight,
Without false vantage or base treachery.
1 *Outlaw.* Why, ne'er repent it, if it were done so.   30
But were you banish'd for so small a fault?
Valentine. I was, and held me glad of such a doom.
2 *Outlaw.* Have you the tongues?
Valentine. My youthful travel therein made me happy,
Or else I often had been miserable.
3 *Outlaw.* By the bare scalp of Robin Hood's fat friar,
This fellow were a king for our wild faction!
1 *Outlaw.* We'll have him.—Sir, a word.

Speed. Master, be one of them ; it 's an honourable kind
of thievery.   40

Valentine. Peace, villain !

2 *Outlaw.* Tell us this : have you any thing to take to ?

Valentine. Nothing but my fortune.

3 *Outlaw.* Know, then, that some of us are gentlemen,
Such as the fury of ungovern'd youth
Thrust from the company of awful men.
Myself was from Verona banished
For practising to steal away a lady,
An heir, and near allied unto the duke.

2 *Outlaw.* And I from Mantua, for a gentleman,   50
Who, in my mood, I stabb'd unto the heart.

1 *Outlaw.* And I for such like petty crimes as these.
But to the purpose—for we cite our faults,
That they may hold excus'd our lawless lives ;
And partly, seeing you are beautified
With goodly shape, and by your own report
A linguist, and a man of such perfection
As we do in our quality much want—

2 *Outlaw.* Indeed, because you are a banish'd man,
Therefore, above the rest, we parley to you.   60
Are you content to be our general ?
To make a virtue of necessity
And live, as we do, in this wilderness ?

3 *Outlaw.* What say'st thou ? wilt thou be of our consort ?
Say ay, and be the captain of us all.
We 'll do thee homage, and be rul'd by thee,
Love thee as our commander and our king.

1 *Outlaw.* But if thou scorn our courtesy, thou diest.

2 *Outlaw.* Thou shalt not live to brag what we have
        offer'd.

Valentine. I take your offer and will live with you,   70
Provided that you do no outrages
On silly women or poor passengers.

3 *Outlaw.* No, we detest such vile base practices.
Come, go with us, we 'll bring thee to our crews,
And show thee all the treasure we have got,
Which, with ourselves, all rest at thy dispose.　　　[*Exeunt.*

SCENE II.　*Milan.　The Court of the Palace.*

Enter PROTEUS.

Proteus. Already have I been false to Valentine,
And now I must be as unjust to Thurio.
Under the colour of commending him,
I have access my own love to prefer ;
But Silvia is too fair, too true, too holy,　　　　.
To be corrupted with my worthless gifts.
When I protest true loyalty to her,
She twits me with my falsehood to my friend ;
When to her beauty I commend my vows,
She bids me think how I have been forsworn　　　　10
In breaking faith with Julia whom I lov'd :
And notwithstanding all her sudden quips,
The least whereof would quell a lover's hope,
Yet, spaniel-like, the more she spurns my love,
The more it grows and fawneth on her still.—
But here comes Thurio. Now must we to her window,
And give some evening music to her ear.

Enter THURIO *and* Musicians.

Thurio. How, now, Sir Proteus, are you crept before us ?
Proteus. Ay, gentle Thurio, for you know that love
Will creep in service where it cannot go.　　　　　20
Thurio. Ay, but I hope, sir, that you love not here.
Proteus. Sir, but I do ; or else I would be hence.
Thurio. Who? Silvia ?
Proteus.　　　　　　　　Ay, Silvia ;—for your sake.
Thurio. I thank you for your own.—Now, gentlemen,
Let 's tune, and to it lustily awhile.

Enter, at a distance, Host, *and* JULIA *in boy's clothes.*

Host. Now, my young guest, methinks you 're allicholly.
I pray you, why is it?

Julia. Marry, mine host, because I cannot be merry.

Host. Come, we 'll have you merry. I 'll bring you where
you shall hear music, and see the gentleman that you asked
for.   31

Julia. But shall I hear him speak?

Host. Ay, that you shall.

Julia. That will be music.   [*Music plays.*

Host. Hark, hark!

Julia. Is he among these?

Host. Ay; but peace! let 's hear 'em.

Song.

> *Who is Silvia? what is she,*
>   *That all our swains commend her?*
> *Holy, fair, and wise is she;*   40
>   *The heaven such grace did lend her,*
> *That she might admired be.*
>
> *Is she kind as she is fair,—*
>   *For beauty lives with kindness?*
> *Love doth to her eyes repair,*
>   *To help him of his blindness,*
> *And, being help'd, inhabits there.*
>
> *Then to Silvia let us sing,*
>   *That Silvia is excelling;*
> *She excels each mortal thing*   50
>   *Upon the dull earth dwelling:*
> *To her let us garlands bring.*

Host. How now! are you sadder than you were before?
How do you, man? the music likes you not.

Julia. You mistake; the musician likes me not.

Host. Why, my pretty youth?

Julia. He plays false, father.

Host. How? out of tune on the strings?

Julia. Not so; but yet so false that he grieves my very
heart-strings. 60

Host. You have a quick ear.

Julia. Ay, I would I were deaf; it makes me have a slow
heart.

Host. I perceive you delight not in music!

Julia. Not a whit, when it jars so.

Host. Hark, what fine change is in the music!

Julia. Ay, that change is the spite.

Host. You would have them always play but one thing?

Julia. I would always have one play but one thing.
But, host, doth this Sir Proteus that we talk on 70
Often resort unto this gentlewoman?

Host. I tell you what Launce, his man, told me;—he loved
her out of all nick.

Julia. Where is Launce?

Host. Gone to seek his dog, which to-morrow, by his master's command, he must carry for a present to his lady.

Julia. Peace, stand aside; the company parts.

Proteus. Sir Thurio, fear not you; I will so plead
That you shall say my cunning drift excels.

Thurio. Where meet we?

Proteus.　　　　　　　At Saint Gregory's well.

Thurio.　　　　　　　　　　　　　　　　Farewell.

[*Exeunt Thurio and Musicians.*

Enter SILVIA *above.*

Proteus. Madam, good even to your ladyship. 81

Silvia. I thank you for your music, gentlemen.
Who is that that spake?

Proteus. One, lady, if you knew his pure heart's truth,
You would quickly learn to know him by his voice.

G

Silvia. Sir Proteus, as I take it.
Proteus. Sir Proteus, gentle lady, and your servant.
Silvia. What 's your will?
Proteus.   That I may compass yours.
Silvia. You have your wish; my will is even this,—
That presently you hie you home to bed.   90
Thou subtle, perjur'd, false, disloyal man!
Think'st thou I am so shallow, so conceitless,
To be seduced by thy flattery,
That hast deceiv'd so many with thy vows?
Return, return, and make thy love amends.
For me, by this pale queen of night I swear,
I am so far from granting thy request
That I despise thee for thy wrongful suit,
And by and by intend to chide myself
Even for this time I spend in talking to thee.   100
    Proteus. I grant, sweet love, that I did love a lady,
But she is dead.
    Julia. [*Aside*] 'T were false, if I should speak it;
For I am sure she is not buried.
    Silvia. Say that she be; yet Valentine thy friend
Survives, to whom, thyself art witness,
I am betroth'd: and art thou not asham'd
To wrong him with thy importunacy?
    Proteus. I likewise hear that Valentine is dead.
    Silvia. And so suppose am I; for in his grave
Assure thyself my love is buried.   110
    Proteus. Sweet lady, let me rake it from the earth.
    Silvia. Go to thy lady's grave and call hers thence,
Or, at the least, in hers sepulchre thine.
    Julia. [*Aside*] He heard not that.
    Proteus. Madam, if your heart be so obdurate,
Vouchsafe me yet your picture for my love,
The picture that is hanging in your chamber.
To that I 'll speak, to that I 'll sigh and weep;

For since the substance of your perfect self
Is else devoted, I am but a shadow,   120
And to your shadow will I make true love.
   Julia. [*Aside*] If 't were a substance, you would, sure, deceive it,
And make it but a shadow, as I am.
   Silvia. I am very loath to be your idol, sir ;
But since your falsehood shall become you well
To worship shadows and adore false shapes,
Send to me in the morning and I 'll send it.
And so, good rest.
   Proteus.   As wretches have o'ernight
That wait for execution in the morn.
                [*Exeunt Proteus and Silvia severally.*
   Julia. Host, will you go?   130
   Host. By my halidom, I was fast asleep.
   Julia. Pray you, where lies Sir Proteus?
   Host. Marry, at my house. Trust me, I think 't is almost day.
   Julia. Not so; but it hath been the longest night
That e'er I watch'd, and the most heaviest.   [*Exeunt.*

Scene III. *The Same.*
Enter Eglamour.

   Eglamour. This is the hour that Madam Silvia
Entreated me to call and know her mind.
There 's some great matter she 'd employ me in.—
Madam, madam!

Enter Silvia *above.*

   Silvia. Who calls?
   Eglamour.   Your servant and your friend ;
One that attends your ladyship's command.
   Silvia. Sir Eglamour, a thousand times good morrow.

Eglamour. As many, worthy lady, to yourself.
According to your ladyship's impose,
I am thus early come to know what service   10
It is your pleasure to command me in.
   Silvia. O Eglamour, thou art a gentleman—
Think not I flatter, for I swear I do not—
Valiant, wise, remorseful, well accomplish'd.
Thou art not ignorant what dear good will
I bear unto the banish'd Valentine;
Nor how my father would enforce me marry
Vain Thurio, whom my very soul abhors.
Thyself hast lov'd; and I have heard thee say
No grief did ever come so near thy heart   20
As when thy lady and thy true love died,
Upon whose grave thou vow'dst pure chastity.
Sir Eglamour, I would to Valentine,
To Mantua, where I hear he makes abode;
And, for the ways are dangerous to pass,
I do desire thy worthy company,
Upon whose faith and honour I repose.
Urge not my father's anger, Eglamour,
But think upon my grief, a lady's grief,
And on the justice of my flying hence,   30
To keep me from a most unholy match,
Which heaven and fortune still rewards with plagues.
I do desire thee, even from a heart
As full of sorrows as the sea of sands,
To bear me company and go with me;
If not, to hide what I have said to thee,
That I may venture to depart alone.
   Eglamour. Madam, I pity much your grievances;
Which since I know they virtuously are plac'd,
I give consent to go along with you,   40
Recking as little what betideth me
As much I wish all good befortune you.
When will you go?

Silvia. This evening coming.

Eglamour. Where shall I meet you?

Silvia. At Friar Patrick's cell,
Where I intend holy confession.

Eglamour. I will not fail your ladyship. Good morrow,
gentle lady.

Silvia. Good morrow, kind Sir Eglamour.

[*Exeunt severally.*

SCENE IV. *The Same.*

Enter LAUNCE, *with his Dog.*

Launce. When a man's servant shall play the cur with him,
look you, it goes hard: one that I brought up of a puppy;
one that I saved from drowning, when three or four of his
blind brothers and sisters went to it. I have taught him,
even as one would say precisely,—thus I would teach a dog.
I was sent to deliver him as a present to Mistress Silvia
from my master; and I came no sooner into the dining-chamber
but he steps me to her trencher and steals her capon's leg.
O, 't is a foul thing when a cur cannot keep himself in all
companies! I would have, as one should say, one that takes
upon him to be a dog indeed, to be, as it were, a dog at all
things. If I had not had more wit than he, to take a fault
upon me that he did, I think verily he had been hanged
for 't; sure as I live, he had suffered for 't. You shall judge.
He thrusts me himself into the company of three or four gentlemanlike dogs, under the duke's table; but all the chamber
smelt him. 'Out with the dog!' says one. 'What cur is
that?' says another. 'Whip him out' says the third. 'Hang
him up' says the duke. I, having been acquainted with the
smell before, knew it was Crab, and goes me to the fellow
that whips the dogs. 'Friend,' quoth I, 'you mean to whip
the dog?' 'Ay, marry, do I,' quoth he. 'You do him the
more wrong,' quoth I; ''t was I did the thing you wot of.'

He makes me no more ado, but whips me out of the chamber. How many masters would do this for his servant? Nay, I 'll be sworn, I have sat in the stocks for puddings he hath stolen, otherwise he had been executed; I have stood on the pillory for geese he hath killed, otherwise he had suffered for 't. Thou thinkest not of this now. Nay, I remember the trick you served me when I took my leave of Madam Silvia. Did not I bid thee still mark me and do as I do? when didst thou see me heave up my leg against a gentlewoman's farthingale? didst thou ever see me do such a trick?

Enter PROTEUS *and* JULIA.

Proteus. Sebastian is thy name? I like thee well
And will employ thee in some service presently.

Julia. In what you please; I 'll do what I can.

Proteus. I hope thou wilt. — [*To Launce*] How now, you
    whoreson peasant!
Where have you been these two days loitering?

Launce. Marry, sir, I carried Mistress Silvia the dog you
bade me.   40

Proteus. And what says she to my little jewel?

Launce. Marry, she says your dog was a cur, and tells you
currish thanks is good enough for such a present.

Proteus. But she received my dog?

Launce. No, indeed, did she not; here have I brought him
back again.

Proteus. What, didst thou offer her this from me?

Launce. Ay, sir; the other squirrel was stolen from me by
the hangman boys in the market-place; and then I offered
her mine own, who is a dog as big as ten of yours, and therefore the gift the greater.   51

Proteus. Go get thee hence, and find my dog again,
Or ne'er return again into my sight.
Away, I say! stay'st thou to vex me here?   [*Exit Launce.*
A slave, that still an end turns me to shame!—

Sebastian, I have entertained thee,
Partly that I have need of such a youth
That can with some discretion do my business—
For 't is no trusting to yond foolish lout—
But chiefly for thy face and thy behaviour,   65
Which, if my augury deceive me not,
Witness good bringing up, fortune, and truth;
Therefore know thou, for this I entertain thee.
Go presently and take this ring with thee,
Deliver it to Madam Silvia.
She lov'd me well deliver'd it to me.
    Julia. It seems you lov'd not her, to leave her token.
She is dead, belike?
    Proteus.   Not so; I think she lives.
    Julia. Alas!
    Proteus. Why dost thou cry, alas!
    Julia.   I cannot choose   70
But pity her.
    Proteus.   Wherefore shouldst thou pity her?
    Julia. Because methinks that she lov'd you as well
As you do love your lady Silvia.
She dreams on him that has forgot her love;
You dote on her that cares not for your love.
'T is pity love should be so contrary;
And thinking on it makes me cry, alas!
    Proteus. Well, give her that ring, and therewithal
This letter. That 's her chamber. Tell my lady
I claim the promise for her heavenly picture.   80
Your message done, hie home unto my chamber,
Where thou shalt find me, sad and solitary.   [*Exit.*
    Julia. How many women would do such a message?
Alas, poor Proteus! thou hast entertain'd
A fox to be the shepherd of thy lambs.—
Alas, poor fool! why do I pity him
That with his very heart despiseth me?

Because he loves her, he despiseth me;
Because I love him, I must pity him.
This ring I gave him when he parted from me,   90
To bind him to remember my good will;
And now am I, unhappy messenger,
To plead for that which I would not obtain,
To carry that which I would have refus'd,
To praise his faith which I would have disprais'd.
I am my master's true-confirmed love,
But cannot be true servant to my master,
Unless I prove false traitor to myself.
Yet will I woo for him, but yet so coldly
As, heaven it knows, I would not have him speed.—   100

Enter SILVIA, *attended.*

Gentlewoman, good day! I pray you, be my mean
To bring me where to speak with Madam Silvia.
    Silvia. What would you with her, if that I be she?
    Julia. If you be she, I do entreat your patience
To hear me speak the message I am sent on.
    Silvia. From whom?
    Julia. From my master, Sir Proteus, madam.
    Silvia. O, he sends you for a picture.
    Julia. Ay, madam.
    Silvia. Ursula, bring my picture there.—   110
Go give your master this; tell him from me,
One Julia, that his changing thoughts forget,
Would better fit his chamber than this shadow.
    Julia. Madam, please you peruse this letter.—
Pardon me, madam, I have unadvis'd
Deliver'd you a paper that I should not;
This is the letter to your ladyship.
    Silvia. I pray thee, let me look on that again.
    Julia. It may not be; good madam, pardon me.
    Silvia. There, hold!   120

I will not look upon your master's lines;
I know they are stuff'd with protestations
And full of new-found oaths, which he will break
As easily as I do tear his paper.

Julia. Madam, he sends your ladyship this ring.

Silvia. The more shame for him that he sends it me;
For I have heard him say a thousand times
His Julia gave it him at his departure.
Though his false finger have profan'd the ring,
Mine shall not do his Julia so much wrong. 120

Julia. She thanks you.

Silvia. What say'st thou?

Julia. I thank you, madam, that you tender her.
Poor gentlewoman! my master wrongs her much.

Silvia. Dost thou know her?

Julia. Almost as well as I do know myself:
To think upon her woes I do protest
That I have wept a hundred several times.

Silvia. Belike she thinks that Proteus hath forsook her.

Julia. I think she doth, and that 's her cause of sorrow.

Silvia. Is she not passing fair? 141

Julia. She hath been fairer, madam, than she is.
When she did think my master lov'd her well,
She, in my judgment, was as fair as you;
But since she did neglect her looking-glass
And threw her sun-expelling mask away,
The air hath starv'd the roses in her cheeks,
And pinch'd the lily-tincture of her face,
That now she is become as black as I.

Silvia. How tall was she? 150

Julia. About my stature; for at Pentecost,
When all our pageants of delight were play'd,
Our youth got me to play the woman's part,
And I was trimm'd in Madam Julia's gown,
Which served me as fit, by all men's judgments,

As if the garment had been made for me;
Therefore I know she is about my height.
And at that time I made her weep agood,
For I did play a lamentable part.
Madam, 't was Ariadne passioning   160
For Theseus' perjury and unjust flight,
Which I so lively acted with my tears
That my poor mistress, moved therewithal,
Wept bitterly; and would I might be dead
If I in thought felt not her very sorrow!
    Silvia. She is beholding to thee, gentle youth.
Alas, poor lady, desolate and left!
I weep myself to think upon thy words.
Here, youth, there is my purse; I give thee this
For thy sweet mistress' sake, because thou lov'st her.   170
Farewell.   [*Exit Silvia, with attendants.*
    Julia. And she shall thank you for 't, if e'er you know
      her.—
A virtuous gentlewoman, mild and beautiful!
I hope my master's suit will be but cold,
Since she respects my mistress' love so much.
Alas, how love can trifle with itself!
Here is her picture. Let me see; I think,
If I had such a tire, this face of mine
Were full as lovely as is this of hers!
And yet the painter flatter'd her a little,   180
Unless I flatter with myself too much.
Her hair is auburn, mine is perfect yellow;
If that be all the difference in his love,
I 'll get me such a colour'd periwig.
Her eyes are grey as glass, and so are mine;
Ay, but her forehead 's low, and mine 's as high.
What should it be that he respects in her
But I can make respective in myself,
If this fond Love were not a blinded god?

Come, shadow, come, and take this shadow up,　　　190
For 't is thy rival.　O thou senseless form,
Thou shalt be worshipp'd, kiss'd, lov'd, and ador'd!
And, were there sense in his idolatry,
My substance should be statue in thy stead.
I 'll use thee kindly for thy mistress' sake,
That us'd me so; or else, by Jove I vow,
I should have scratch'd out your unseeing eyes,
To make my master out of love with thee!　　　[*Exit.*

ITALIAN LADIES (AFTER VECELLIO).

ABBEY OF SANT' AMBROGIO, MILAN.

ACT V.

SCENE I. *Milan. An Abbey.*

Enter EGLAMOUR.

Eglamour. The sun begins to gild the western sky;
And now it is about the very hour
That Silvia, at Friar Patrick's cell, should meet me.

She will not fail, for lovers break not hours,
Unless it be to come before their time,
So much they spur their expedition.
See where she comes.—

Enter SILVIA.

Lady, a happy evening!
Silvia. Amen, amen! Go on, good Eglamour,
Out at the postern by the abbey-wall.
I fear I am attended by some spies.   10
  Eglamour. Fear not: the forest is not three leagues off;
If we recover that, we are sure enough.   [*Exeunt.*

SCENE II. *The Same. The Duke's Palace.*

Enter THURIO, PROTEUS, *and* JULIA.

Thurio. Sir Proteus, what says Silvia to my suit?
Proteus. O, sir, I find her milder than she was;
And yet she takes exceptions at your person.
Thurio. What, that my leg is too long?
Proteus. No; that it is too little.
Thurio. I 'll wear a boot, to make it somewhat rounder.
Julia. [*Aside*] But love will not be spurr'd to what it
  loathes.
Thurio. What says she to my face?
Proteus. She says it is a fair one.
Thurio. Nay, then, the wanton lies; my face is black.   10
Proteus. But pearls are fair; and the old saying is,
Black men are pearls in beauteous ladies' eyes.
Julia. [*Aside*] 'T is true, such pearls as put out ladies'
  eyes;
For I had rather wink than look on them.
Thurio. How likes she my discourse?
Proteus. Ill, when you talk of war.
Thurio. But well, when I discourse of love and peace?

Julia. [*Aside*] But better, indeed, when you hold your peace.

Thurio. What says she to my valour?

Proteus. O, sir, she makes no doubt of that.   20

Julia. [*Aside*] She needs not, when she knows it cowardice.

Thurio. What says she to my birth?

Proteus. That you are well derived.

Julia. [*Aside*] True; from a gentleman to a fool.

Thurio. Considers she my possessions?

Proteus. O, ay; and pities them.

Thurio. Wherefore?

Julia. [*Aside*] That such an ass should owe them.

Proteus. That they are out by lease.

Julia. Here comes the duke.   30

Enter DUKE.

Duke. How now, Sir Proteus! how now, Thurio!
Which of you saw Sir Eglamour of late?

Thurio. Not I.

Proteus.   Nor I.

Duke.   Saw you my daughter?

Proteus.   Neither.

Duke. Why then,
She 's fled unto that peasant Valentine,
And Eglamour is in her company.
'T is true; for Friar Laurence met them both,
As he in penance wander'd through the forest.
Him he knew well, and guess'd that it was she,
But, being mask'd, he was not sure of it;   40
Besides, she did intend confession
At Patrick's cell this even, and there she was not.
These likelihoods confirm her flight from hence.
Therefore, I pray you, stand not to discourse,
But mount you presently and meet with me

Upon the rising of the mountain-foot
That leads toward Mantua, whither they are fled.
Dispatch, sweet gentlemen, and follow me.   [*Exit.*
     Thurio. Why, this it is to be a peevish girl,
That flies her fortune when it follows her.   50
I 'll after, more to be reveng'd on Eglamour
Than for the love of reckless Silvia.   [*Exit.*
     Proteus. And I will follow, more for Silvia's love
Than hate of Eglamour that goes with her.   [*Exit.*
     Julia. And I will follow, more to cross that love
Than hate for Silvia, that is gone for love.   [*Exit.*

SCENE III.   *The Forest.*

Enter Outlaws *with* SILVIA.

     1 *Outlaw.* Come, come,
Be patient; we must bring you to our captain.
     Silvia. A thousand more mischances than this one
Have learn'd me how to brook this patiently.
     2 *Outlaw.* Come, bring her away.
     1 *Outlaw.* Where is the gentleman that was with her?
     3 *Outlaw.* Being nimble-footed, he hath outrun us,
But Moyses and Valerius follow him.
Go thou with her to the west end of the wood;
There is our captain. We 'll follow him that 's fled;   10
The thicket is beset; he cannot scape.
     1 *Outlaw.* Come, I must bring you to our captain's cave.
Fear not; he bears an honourable mind,
And will not use a woman lawlessly.
     Silvia. O Valentine, this I endure for thee!   [*Exeunt.*

SCENE IV.   *Another Part of the Forest.*

Enter VALENTINE.

     Valentine. How use doth breed a habit in a man!
These shadowy, desert, unfrequented woods,

I better brook than flourishing peopled towns:
Here can I sit alone, unseen of any,
And to the nightingale's complaining notes
Tune my distresses and record my woes.
O thou that dost inhabit in my breast,
Leave not the mansion so long tenantless,
Lest, growing ruinous, the building fall
And leave no memory of what it was!   10
Repair me with thy presence, Silvia;
Thou gentle nymph, cherish thy forlorn swain!—
What halloing and what stir is this to-day?
'T is sure, my mates, that make their wills their law,
Have some unhappy passenger in chase.
They love me well; yet I have much to do
To keep them from uncivil outrages.
Withdraw thee, Valentine; who 's this comes here?

Enter PROTEUS, SILVIA, *and* JULIA.

Proteus. Madam, this service I have done for you,
Though you respect not aught your servant doth,   20
To hazard life and rescue you from him
That would have forc'd your honour and your love.
Vouchsafe me, for my meed, but one fair look;
A smaller boon than this I cannot beg,
And less than this, I am sure, you cannot give.
  Valentine. [*Aside*] How like a dream is this I see and hear!
Love, lend me patience to forbear awhile.
  Silvia. O miserable, unhappy that I am!
  Proteus. Unhappy were you, madam, ere I came;
But by my coming I have made you happy.   30
  Silvia. By thy approach thou mak'st me most unhappy.
  Julia. [*Aside*] And me, when he approacheth to your
    presence.
  Silvia. Had I been seized by a hungry lion,
I would have been a breakfast to the beast,

Rather than have false Proteus rescue me.
O, Heaven be judge how I love Valentine,
Whose life 's as tender to me as my soul!
And full as much, for more there cannot be,
I do detest false perjur'd Proteus.
Therefore be gone, solicit me no more.　　　　40
　　Proteus. What dangerous action, stood it next to death,
Would I not undergo for one calm look!
O, 't is the curse in love, and still approv'd,
When women cannot love where they 're belov'd!
　　Silvia. When Proteus cannot love where he 's belov'd.
Read over Julia's heart, thy first best love,
For whose dear sake thou didst then rend thy faith
Into a thousand oaths; and all those oaths
Descended into perjury, to love me.
Thou hast no faith left now, unless thou 'dst two;　　　50
And that 's far worse than none : better have none
Than plural faith, which is too much by one.
Thou counterfeit to thy true friend!
　　Proteus.　　　　　　　　In love
Who respects friend?
　　Silvia.　　　　　All men but Proteus.
　　Proteus. Nay, if the gentle spirit of moving words
Can no way change you to a milder form,
I 'll woo you like a soldier, at arms' end,
And love you 'gainst the nature of love,—force ye.
　　Silvia. O heaven!
　　Proteus.　　　　I 'll force thee yield to my desire.
　　Valentine. Ruffian, let go that rude uncivil touch,　　　60
Thou friend of an ill fashion!
　　Proteus.　　　　　　Valentine!
　　Valentine. Thou common friend, that 's without faith or
　　　love,—
For such is a friend now,—treacherous man!
Thou hast beguil'd my hopes; nought but mine eye
　　　　　　　　　H

Could have persuaded me.   Now I dare not say
I have one friend alive; thou wouldst disprove me.
Who should be trusted, when one's own right hand
Is perjur'd to the bosom?   Proteus,
I am sorry I must never trust thee more,
But count the world a stranger for thy sake.   70
The private wound is deep'st.   O time most accurst,
'Mongst all foes that a friend should be the worst!
    Proteus. My shame and guilt confounds me.—
Forgive me, Valentine.   If hearty sorrow
Be a sufficient ransom for offence,
I tender 't here; I do as truly suffer
As e'er I did commit.
    Valentine.   Then I am paid;
And once again I do receive thee honest.
Who by repentance is not satisfied
Is nor of heaven nor earth, for these are pleas'd.   80
By penitence the Eternal's wrath 's appeas'd;
And, that my love may appear plain and free,
All that was mine in Silvia I give thee.
    Julia. O me unhappy!   [*Swoons.*
    Proteus. Look to the boy.
    Valentine. Why, boy! why, wag! how now! what 's the mat-
ter?   Look up; speak.
    Julia. O good sir, my master charged me to deliver a
ring to Madam Silvia, which, out of my neglect, was never
done.   90
    Proteus. Where is that ring, boy?
    Julia.   Here 't is; this is it.
    Proteus. How! let me see.—
Why, this is the ring I gave to Julia.
    Julia. O, cry you mercy, sir, I have mistook:
This is the ring you sent to Silvia.
    Proteus. But how cam'st thou by this ring?   At my depart
I gave this unto Julia.

Julia. And Julia herself did give it me;
And Julia herself hath brought it hither.
Proteus. How! Julia!   100
Julia. Behold her that gave aim to all thy oaths,
And entertain'd 'em deeply in her heart.
How oft hast thou with perjury cleft the root!
O Proteus, let this habit make thee blush!
Be thou asham'd that I have took upon me
Such an immodest raiment, if shame live
In a disguise of love.
It is the lesser blot, modesty finds,
Women to change their shapes than men their minds.
Proteus. Than men their minds! 't is true. O heaven!
      were man   110
But constant, he were perfect. That one error
Fills him with faults, makes him run through all the sins;
Inconstancy falls off ere it begins.
What is in Silvia's face, but I may spy
More fresh in Julia's with a constant eye?
Valentine. Come, come, a hand from either.
Let me be blest to make this happy close;
'T were pity two such friends should be long foes.
Proteus. Bear witness, heaven, I have my wish for ever.
Julia. And I mine.   120

      Enter Outlaws, *with* DUKE *and* THURIO.

Outlaws. A prize, a prize, a prize!
Valentine. Forbear, forbear, I say! it is my lord the duke.—
Your grace is welcome to a man disgrac'd,
Banished Valentine.
Duke.   Sir Valentine!
Thurio. Yonder is Silvia; and Silvia 's mine.
Valentine. Thurio, give back, or else embrace thy death;
Come not within the measure of my wrath.
Do not name Silvia thine; if once again,

Verona shall not hold thee.   Here she stands:
Take but possession of her with a touch;   130
I dare thee but to breathe upon my love.
     Thurio. Sir Valentine, I care not for her, I.
I hold him but a fool that will endanger
His body for a girl that loves him not;
I claim her not, and therefore she is thine.
     Duke. The more degenerate and base art thou,
To make such means for her as thou hast done,
And leave her on such slight conditions.—
Now, by the honour of my ancestry,
I do applaud thy spirit, Valentine,   140
And think thee worthy of an empress' love.
Know then, I here forget all former griefs,
Cancel all grudge, repeal thee home again.
Plead a new state in thy unrivall'd merit,
To which I thus subscribe : Sir Valentine,
Thou art a gentleman and well deriv'd;   ‘
Take thou thy Silvia, for thou hast deserv'd her.
     Valentine. I thank your grace; the gift hath made me
          happy.
I now beseech you, for your daughter's sake,
To grant one boon that I shall ask of you.   150
     Duke. I grant it, for thine own, whate'er it be.
     Valentine. These banish'd men that I have kept withal
Are men endued with worthy qualities.
Forgive them what they have committed here
And let them be recall'd from their exile:
They are reformed, civil, full of good,
And fit for great employment, worthy lord.
     Duke. Thou hast prevail'd; I pardon them and thee:
Dispose of them as thou know'st their deserts.
Come, let us go; we will include all jars   160
With triumphs, mirth, and rare solemnity.
     Valentine. And, as we walk along, I dare be bold

With our discourse to make your grace to smile.
What think you of this page, my lord?
   Duke. I think the boy hath grace in him; he blushes.
   Valentine. I warrant you, my lord, more grace than boy.
   Duke. What mean you by that saying?
   Valentine. Please you, I 'll tell you as we pass along,
That you will wonder what hath fortuned.—
Come, Proteus; 't is your penance but to hear   170
The story of your loves discovered.
That done, our day of marriage shall be yours;
One feast, one house, one mutual happiness.   [*Exeunt.*

CUPID (AFTER FRANCESCO ALBANO).

VERONA.

NOTES.

ABBREVIATIONS USED IN THE NOTES.

Abbott (or Gr.), Abbott's *Shakespearian Grammar* (third edition).
A. S., Anglo-Saxon.
A. V., Authorized Version of the Bible (1611).
B. and F., Beaumont and Fletcher.
B. J., Ben Jonson.
Camb. ed., "Cambridge edition" of Shakespeare, edited by Clark and Wright. •
Cf. (*confer*), compare.
Clarke, "Cassell's Illustrated Shakespeare," edited by Charles and Mary Cowden-Clarke (London, n. d.).
Coll., Collier (second edition).
Coll. MS., Manuscript Corrections of Second Folio, edited by Collier.
D., Dyce (second edition).
H., Hudson (" Harvard" edition).
Halliwell, J. O. Halliwell (folio ed. of Shakespeare).
Id. (*idem*), the same.
K., Knight (second edition).
Nares, *Glossary*, edited by Halliwell and Wright (London, 1859).
Prol., Prologue.
S., Shakespeare.
Schmidt, A. Schmidt's *Shakespeare-Lexicon* (Berlin, 1874).
Sr., Singer.
St., Staunton.
Theo., Theobald.
V., Verplanck.
W., R. Grant White.
Walker, Wm. Sidney Walker's *Critical Examination of the Text of Shakespeare* (London, 1860).
Warb., Warburton.
Wb., Webster's Dictionary (revised quarto edition of 1879).
Worc., Worcester's Dictionary (quarto edition).

The abbreviations of the names of Shakespeare's Plays will be readily understood; as *T. N.* for *Twelfth Night*, *Cor.* for *Coriolanus*, 3 *Hen. VI.* for *The Third Part of King Henry the Sixth*, etc. *P. P.* refers to *The Passionate Pilgrim*; *V. and A.* to *Venus and Adonis*; *L. C.* to *Lover's Complaint*; and *Sonn.* to the *Sonnets.*

When the abbreviation of the name of a play is followed by a reference to *page*, Rolfe's edition of the play is meant.
The numbers of the lines (except for the present play) are those of the " Globe " ed.

NOTES.

ITALIAN NOBLEMAN (AFTER HOGHENBURG).

ACT I.

DRAMATIS PERSONÆ.—The 1st folio (cf. *Oth.* p. 153) has the following list at the end of the play:

The Names of all the Actors.

Duke: *Father to* Siluia.

Valentine. } *the two Gentlemen.*
Protheus. }

Anthonio: father to Protheus.

Thurio: a foolish riuall to Valentine.

Eglamoure: Agent for Siluia in her escape.

Host: where Iulia lodges.

Out-lawes with Valentine.

Speed: a clownish seruant to Valentine.

Launce: the like to Protheus.

Panthion: seruant to Antonio.

Iulia: beloued of Protheus.

Siluia: beloued of Valentine.

Lucetta: waighting-woman to Iulia.

Protheus is the old way of spelling *Proteus.* Steevens quotes Gascoigne, *Princely Pleasures at Kenelworth Castle,* 1587 : " *Protheus* appeared, sitting on a dolphyn's back ;" and Barclay, *Eclogues:* "Like as Protheus oft chaungeth his nature." Clarke remarks : "To the fickle, unstable, changeable character thus designated, we have always felt a certain propriety in the poet's assigning the name of Proteus ; a sea-deity, whose power of changing his shape has become proverbial as a type of changeableness."

On the spelling of the name, cf. *Anthonio* for *Antonio ;* and on the pronunciation of *th,* cf. *A. Y. L.* p. 179 (note on *Goats*), *Much Ado,* p. 136 (on *Nothing*), and *L. L. L.* p. 128 (on *Dramatis Personæ*). Malone says that Lydgate has *Thelephus* and *Anthenor ;* and in the old translation of the *Gesta Romanorum,* 1580, we find *Athalanta* for *Atalanta.*

Panthion occurs in the folio only in the list of "Actors" and in the stage-directions. In the text (i. 3. 1) it is "*Panthino*" or (i. 3. 76) "*Panthmo,*" which is obviously a misprint for "*Panthino.*" In the heading of i. 3 we also find "*Enter Antonio and Panthino.*"

SCENE I. — 2. *Home-keeping youth have ever homely wits.* Steevens quotes Milton, *Comus,* 748 :

" It is for homely features to keep home ;
They had their name thence."

8. *Shapeless.* "The expression is fine, as implying that idleness prevents the giving any form or character to the manners " (Warb.).

18. *Beadsman.* One who prays in behalf of another ; from the A. S. *bead,* prayer (see Wb.). Cf. *Hen. V.* iv. 1. 315 :

" Five hundred poor I have in yearly pay,
Who twice a day their wither'd hands hold up
Toward heaven, to pardon blood."

22. *Leander.* Malone sees an allusion to the poem of Musæus on Hero and Leander, translated by Marlowe ; but this was not printed till 1598, though entered on the Stationers' Registers in 1593. The story was doubtless familiar to the poet from his schooldays. For other allusions to it, cf. iii. 1. 120 below, *Much Ado,* v. 2. 30, *A. Y. L.* iv. 1. 100, and *M. N. D.* v. 1. 198.

25. *For.* Changed in the Coll. MS. to "but," and by H. to "and." D. says : "The old text, if right, must be explained : ' Yes, it is certainly true ; for you are not merely, as he was, over shoes in love, but even over

boots in love, and yet,' etc.—*for you are* corresponding to the former *For he was.*"

27. *Give me not the boots.* "A proverbial expression, though now disused, signifying, don't make a laughing-stock of me, don't play upon me. The French have a phrase, *Bailler foin en corne,* which Cotgrave thus interprets: 'To give one the boots; to sell him a bargain'" (Theo.). Steevens is doubtful whether the expression took its origin from a Warwickshire sport, in which the victim was "laid on a bench and slapped on the breech with a pair of boots," or from the ancient engine of torture known as the *boots.*

34. *However.* However it may turn out, in any case.

37. *By your circumstance.* "*Circumstance* here means conduct; in the preceding line, circumstantial deduction" (Malone).

42. *As in the sweetest bud,* etc. Malone quotes *Sonn.* 70. 7 : "For canker vice the sweetest buds doth love." On *canker*=canker-worm, cf. *M. N. D.* p. 150.

52. *Fond.* Doting. When the word is used in this sense, it often carries with it the more common old meaning of foolish. Cf. iv. 4. 189 below; and see *M. N. D.* p. 163, note on *Fond pageant.*

53. *Road.* Port, haven; as in ii. 4. 185 below.

57. *To Milan.* Changed in the 2d folio and some modern eds. to "At Milan;" but the meaning is *by letters to Milan.* Malone conjectured "To Milan !—let me hear," etc.

61. *Bechance.* Cf. *R. of L.* 976 : "Let there bechance him pitiful mischances," etc.

65. *I leave myself.* The folios have "love" for *leave;* corrected by Pope.

71. *Embark for Milan.* According to Elze, Milan and Verona were actually connected by canals in the 16th century.

73. *Sheep.* For the play on *ship* and *sheep,* which seem to have been pronounced nearly alike, cf. *C. of E.* iv. 1. 93 and *L. L. L.* ii. 1. 219.

83. *It shall go hard but I 'll,* etc. Cf. *M. of V.* iii. 1. 75 : "It shall go hard but I will better the instruction," etc.

95. *Laced mutton.* Schmidt says: "According to glossarists and commentators, a cant term for a prostitute; but probably only =woman's flesh, a petticoat, a smock." Cotgrave defines *laced mutton* by "une garse, putain, fille de joye;" and the quotations given by Steevens, Malone, and others show plainly enough that it commonly meant a loose woman rather than a "straight-laced" one. In the present passage, however, it may have the sense that Schmidt gives it; or, as W. better puts it, "a fine piece of woman's flesh." St., who takes it in the ordinary sense, says that "the only palliation for Speed's application of it is that in reality it was not the lady, but her waiting-maid, to whom he gave the letter."

99. *You were best.* It would be best for you. Cf. i. 3. 24 below. Gr. 230, 352.

101. *Astray.* Theo. has "a stray." The pointing is that of the folios. The Camb. ed. gives : "Nay : in that you are astray, 't were best," etc.

105. *Pinfold.* Cf. *Lear,* ii. 2. 9: "in Lipsbury pinfold;" and Milton, *Comus,* 7: "Confin'd and pester'd in this pinfold here."

110. *That 's noddy.* For the quibble, Reed compares *Wit's Private Wealth,* 1612: "give her a nod, but follow her not, lest you prove a noddy." It does not seem necessary to follow the old eds. in printing "I" for *ay* (as they uniformly do), in order to make the joke obvious.

121. *Beshrew me.* A mild form of imprecation, often used, as here, merely to emphasize an assertion. Cf. ii. 4. 73 below.

133. *In telling your mind.* That is, when you tell her your mind, or make suit to her. The 2d folio changes *your* to "her," and the Coll. MS. to "you her."

135. *What, said she nothing?* The Camb. ed. reads "What said she? nothing?"

137. *Testerned me.* Given me a *tester, testern,* or sixpence. Cf. 2 *Hen. IV.* iii. 2. 296: "there 's a tester for you," etc. The 1st folio misprints "cestern'd;" corrected in the 2d folio.

140. *Wrack.* The only spelling in the early eds. Cf. the rhymes in *V. and A.* 558, *R. of L.* 841, 965, *Sonn.* 126. 5, and *Macb.* v. 5. 51.

142. *Being destin'd to a drier death on shore.* That is, to be hanged. Cf. *Temp.* i. 1. 31 fol. and *Id.* v. 1. 217.

Clarke says: "It is worthy of remark that Speed's flippancy exceeds the licensed pertness of a jester, and degenerates into impertinence when speaking with Proteus; thus subtly conveying the dramatist's intention in the character itself. Had Proteus not been the mean, unworthy man he is, as gentleman and lover, Speed had not dared to twit him so broadly with his niggardly and reluctant recompense, or to speak in such free terms of the lady Proteus addresses."

SCENE II.—**5.** *Parle.* Parley, talk; elsewhere only (literally or figuratively) in the military sense of a parley, or conference with regard to terms of truce or peace. Cf. *K. John,* ii. 1. 205, 226, *Hen. V.* iii. 3. 2, etc.

7. *Please you repeat their names,* etc. Cf. *M. of V.* i. 2. 39: "I pray thee, overname them; and as thou namest them, I will describe them," etc. See also p. 37 above.

19. *Censure.* Pass judgment; not elsewhere followed by *on.* For the transitive use in this sense, cf. *Much Ado,* p. 139, or *Lear,* p. 225. Hanmer changes *thus* to "pass." The Coll. MS. has

> "That I, unworthy body, as I can,
> Should censure thus a loving gentleman;"

but *censure thus on* is confirmed by the *on* in the next speech.

30. *Fire.* Pope reads "The fire;" and Johnson "that is" for *that 's;* but *fire* is sometimes a dissyllable. See Gr. 480.

41. *Broker.* Go-between. Cf. *K. John,* ii. 1. 582: "This bawd, this broker," etc. See also *Ham.* p. 191.

50. *O'erlook'd.* Looked over, perused; as in *M. N. D.* ii. 2. 121:

> "And leads me to your eyes, where I o'erlook
> Love's stories written in love's richest book,"

See also *Lear,* v. 1. 50, *Hen. V.* ii. 4. 90, etc.

53. *What fool is she.* The folios, except the 4th, print "what ' foole," and some modern eds. give "what a fool;" but the article was sometimes omitted in such cases. Cf. *J. C.* i. 3. 42: " Cassius, what night is this !" For other examples, see Gr. 86.

62. *Angerly.* Cf. *K. John,* iv. 1. 82 and *Macb.* iii. 5. 1. See also Gr. 447.

68. *Stomach.* There is a play upon the senses of wrath (see *Lear,* p. 254) and hunger; also upon *meat* (pronounced *mate*) and *maid.* Cf. the quibble on *baits* and *beats* in *IV. T.* ii. 3. 92, etc.

76, 77. The play on the two senses of *lie* is obvious.

81. *Set.* That is, set to music. Julia plays upon the word in her reply.

83. *Light o' love.* For another allusion to this popular old tune, see *Much Ado,* iii. 4. 44: " Clap 's into ' Light o' love ;' that goes without a burden."

94. *Descant.* Malone explains this as "variations," and Schmidt as "treble ;" but W. shows that the word means the adding of other parts to the "ground" or theme. He quotes Phillips, *New World of Words :* "Descant (in Musick) signifies the Art of Composing in several parts," etc. Florio defines *Contrapunto* as "a counterpoint ; also a descant in musicke or singing." Cf. the figurative use of the word in *Rich. III.* iii. 7. 49 : " For on that ground I 'll make a holy descant."

95. *Mean.* Tenor. Cf. *IV. T.* iv. 3. 46 : "they are most of them means and bases ;" and *L. L. L.* v. 2. 328 :

> "nay, he can sing
> A mean most meanly," etc.

97. *I bid the base.* Alluding to the game of prison-base, in which the fastest runner wins. Cf. *V. and A.* 303 : " To bid the wind a base he now prepares " (that is, challenges the wind to run a race) ; and *Cymb.* v. 3. 20 :

> "lads more like to run
> The country base than to commit such slaughter."

See also Spenser, *Shep. Kal.* Oct. 5 : " In rymes, in ridles, and in bydding base."

99. *Coil.* Ado, "fuss." Cf. *C. of E.* iii. 1. 48 : " What a coil is there, Dromio ?" See also *Much Ado,* p. 146, or *M. N. D.* p. 168.

Protestation is metrically five syllables. Gr. 479.

102. *Best pleas'd.* The Coll. MS. has "pleas'd better."

104. *Nay, would I,* etc. St. has little doubt that this line is part of Lucetta's side speech. It is inconsistent, he says, that Julia should reply to what is spoken *aside,* and the reply is moreover without meaning in her mouth. If it belongs to Julia, the meaning evidently must be that she would be glad to get another such letter. She has overheard what Lucetta has said, and the repetition of *anger'd* is ironical.

108. *Several.* Separate. Cf. *Temp.* p. 131.

115. *Throughly.* Used by S. interchangeably with *thoroughly.* See *M. of V.* p. 144, note on *Thoroughfares.*

121. *Fearful-hanging.* The hyphen was first inserted by Delius.

124. *Forlorn.* Accented on the first syllable (as in v. 4. 12 below) because preceding a noun so accented. Cf. *Sonn.* 33. 7 : "And from the

forlorn world his visage hide." On the other hand, see *R. of L.* 1500 :
" And whom she finds forlorn she doth lament ;" and *L. L. L.* v. 2. 805 :
" To some forlorn and naked hermitage." For many similar examples,
see Schmidt, p. 1413 fol.

126. *Sith.* Since. Cf. *Cor.* p. 236 (note on *Sithence*), or Gr. 132.
134. *Respect them.* Care about them. Cf. *Rich. III.* i. 3. 296 :

> "*Gloster.* What doth she say, my Lord of Buckingham?
> *Buckingham.* Nothing that I respect, my gracious lord."

136. *For catching cold.* That is, for fear of catching cold. Cf. *Sonn.*
52. 4 :

> "So am I as the rich, whose blessed key
> Can bring him to his sweet up-locked treasure,
> The which he will not every hour survey,
> For blunting the fine point of seldom pleasure ;'

and 2 *Hen. VI.* iv. 1. 74 :

> "Now will I dam up this thy yawning mouth,
> For swallowing the treasure of the realm."

137. *A month's mind.* An earnest wish or longing. The expression
is said to have originated in the periodical celebration of mass for the
souls of the dead. Grey quotes Strype, *Memorials :* " Was the month's
mind of Sir William Laxton, who died the last month, his hearse burning with wax, and the morrow-mass celebrated," etc. Puttenham, in his
Arte of Poesie, says that poetical lamentations were chiefly used " at the
burials of the dead, also at month's minds, and longer times." Schmidt
explains the phrase here as =" a woman's longing." Steevens suggests
" monthes " for the measure, and W. reads " moneth's." The word is evidently dissyllabic, as Schmidt makes it in 3 *Hen. VI.* ii. 5. 38 : " So min-
utes, hours, days, months, and years."

139. *Wink.* Shut my eyes ; as often. Cf. *Cymb.* p. 182.

SCENE III.—1. *Sad.* Serious. Cf. *Much Ado*, i. 1. 185 : " Speak you
this with a sad brow ?" and see our ed. p. 121.

6. *Of slender reputation.* " That is, who are thought slightly of, are of
little consequence " (Steevens).

9. *Some to discover islands far away.* " In Shakespeare's time, voyages
for the discovery of the islands of America were much in vogue ; and we
find, in the journals of the travellers of that time, that the sons of noblemen, and of others of the best families in England, went very frequently
on these adventures " (Warb.). Gifford, in his *Memoirs of Ben Jonson,*
prefixed to his edition of that dramatist, says : " The long reign of Elizabeth, though sufficiently agitated to keep the mind alert, was yet a season
of comparative stability and peace. The nobility, who had been nursed
in domestic turbulence, for which there was now no place, and the more
active spirits among the gentry, for whom entertainment could no longer
be found in feudal grandeur and hospitality, took advantage of the diver-
sity of employment happily opened, and spread themselves in every di-
rection. They put forth, in the language of Shakspere,

'Some, to the wars, to try their fortunes there;
Some, to discover islands far away;
Some, to the studious universities;'

and the effect of these various pursuits was speedily discernible. The feelings narrowed and embittered in household feuds, expanded and purified themselves in distant warfare, and a high sense of honour and generosity, and chivalrous valour, ran with electric speed from bosom to bosom, on the return of the first adventurers in the Flemish campaigns ; while the wonderful reports of discoveries, by the intrepid mariners who opened the route since so successfully pursued, faithfully committed to writing, and acting at once upon the cupidity and curiosity of the times, produced an inconceivable effect in diffusing a thirst for novelties among a people who, no longer driven in hostile array to destroy one another, and combat for interests in which they took little concern, had leisure for looking around them, and consulting their own amusement."

13. *Importune.* Accented by S. on the second syllable. Cf. *Ham.* p. 190. Gr. 490.

15. *Impeachment.* Reproach, discredit. Cf. the verb in *M. N. D.* ii. 1. 214: "You do impeach your modesty too much," etc.

24. *Were I best.* Would it be best for me. See on i. 1. 99 above.

27. *The emperor.* "S. has been guilty of no mistake in placing the emperor's court at Milan. Several of the first German emperors held their courts there occasionally, it being at that time their immediate property, and the chief town of their Italian dominions. Some of them were crowned kings of Italy at Milan before they received the imperial crown at Rome. Nor has the poet fallen into any contradiction by giving a duke to Milan at the same time that the emperor held his court there. The first dukes of that and all the other great cities in Italy were not sovereign princes, as they afterwards became, but were merely governors, or viceroys, under the emperors, and removable at their pleasure " (Steevens).

30. *There shall he practise tilts and tournaments.* "St. Palaye, in his *Memoirs of Chivalry,* says that, in their private castles, the gentlemen *practised* the exercises which would prepare them for the public tournaments. This refers to the period which appears to have terminated some half-century before the time of Elizabeth, when real warfare was conducted with express reference to the laws of knighthood ; and the tourney, with all its magnificent array,—its minstrels, its heralds, and its damosels in lofty towers,—had its hard blows, its wounds, and sometimes its deaths. There were the 'Joustes à outrance,' or the 'Joustes mortelles et à champ,' of Froissart. But the 'tournaments' that Shakspere sends Proteus to 'practise' were the 'Joustes of Peace,'the 'Joustes à plaisance,' the tournaments of gay pennons and pointless lances. They had all the gorgeousness of the old knightly encounters, but they appear to have been regarded only as courtly pastimes, and not as serious preparations for 'a well-foughten field.' One or two instances from the annals of these times will at least amuse our readers, if they do not quite satisfy them that these combats were as harmless to the combatants as the fierce encounters between other less noble actors—the heroes of the stage.

"On Whitsun Monday, 1581, a most magnificent tournament was held in the Tilt-yard at Westminster, in honour of the Dauphin, and other noblemen and gentlemen of France, who had arrived as commissioners to the queen. Holinshed describes the proceedings respecting this 'Triumph' at great length. A magnificent gallery was erected for the queen and her court, which was called by the combatants the fortress of perfect beauty; 'and not without cause, forasmuch as her highness would be there included.' Four gentlemen—the Earl of Arundel, the Lord Windsor, Mr. Philip Sidney, and Mr. Fulke Greville—calling themselves the foster-children of Desire, laid claim to this fortress, and vowed to withstand all who should dare to oppose them. Their challenge being accepted by certain gentlemen of the court, they proceeded (in gorgeous apparel, and attended by squires and attendants richly dressed) forthwith to the tilt, and on the following day to the tourney, where they behaved nobly and bravely, but, at length, submitted to the queen, acknowledging that they ought not to have accompanied Desire by Violence, and concluding a long speech, full of the compliments of the day, by declaring themselves thenceforth slaves to the 'Fortress of Perfect Beautie.' These 'Courtlie triumphes' were arranged and conducted in the most costly manner. The queen's gallery was painted in imitation of stone and covered with ivy and garlands of flowers; cannons were fired with perfumed powder; the dresses of the knights and courtiers were of the richest stuffs, and covered with precious stones; and moving mounts, costly chariots, and many other devices were introduced to give effect to the scene.

"In the reign of Elizabeth there were annual exercises of arms, which were first commenced by Sir Henry Lee. This worthy knight made a vow to appear armed in the Tilt-yard at Westminster on the 27th November (the anniversary of the queen's accession) in every year, until disabled by age, where he offered to tilt with all comers, in honour of Her Majesty's accession. He continued the queen's champion until the thirty-third year of her reign, when, having arrived at the sixtieth year of his age, he resigned in favour of George, Earl of Cumberland, who was invested in the office with much form and solemnity in 1590. It was on the 27th November in that year, that Sir Henry Lee, having performed his devoirs in the lists for the last time, and with much applause, accompanied by the Earl of Cumberland, presented himself before the queen, who was seated in her gallery overlooking the lists, and, kneeling on one knee, humbly besought Her Majesty to accept the Earl of Cumberland for her knight, to continue the yearly exercises which he was compelled, from infirmities of age, himself to relinquish. The queen graciously accepting the offer, the old knight presented his armour at Her Majesty's feet, and then assisting in fastening the armour of the earl, he mounted him on his horse. This ceremony being performed, he put upon his own person a side coat of 'black velvet pointed under the arm, and covered his head (in lieu of a helmet) with a buttoned cap of the country fashion.' Then, whilst music was heard proceeding from a magnificent temple which had been erected for the occasion, he presented to the queen, through the hands of three beautiful maidens, a veil curiously wrought, and richly adorned, and other gifts of great magnificence, and declared that, although his youth and strength had decayed, his duty, faith, and love remained perfect as ever ; his hands, instead of wielding the lance, should now be held up in prayer for Her Majesty's welfare ; and he trusted she would allow him to be her Beadsman, now that he had ceased to incur knightly perils in her service. But the queen complimented him upon his gallantry, and desired that he would attend the future annual jousts, and direct the knights in their proceedings ; for indeed his virtue and valour in arms were declared by all to be deserving of command. In the course of the good old knight's career of ' virtue and valour in arms,' he was joined by many companions, anxious to distinguish themselves in all courtly and chivalrous exercises. One duke, nineteen earls, twenty-seven barons, four knights of the garter, and above one hundred and fifty other knights and esquires, are stated to have taken part in these annual feats of arms.

" If Shakspere had not looked upon these ' Annual Exercises of Arms,' when he thought of the tournaments ' in the emperor's court,' he had probably been admitted to the Tilt-yard at Kenilworth, on some occasion of magnificent display by the proud Leicester " (K.).

44. *And—in good time!* And here he comes most opportunely ! "*In good time* was the old expression when something happened which suited the thing in hand, as the French say, *à propos* " (Johnson). Cf. *Rich. III.* ii. 1. 45, iii. 1. 24, 95, iii. 4. 22, etc.

Break with him. Broach the matter to him. See *Much Ado,* p. 125. Cf. iii. 1. 59 below.

48. *Applaud.* Approve ; as in v. 4. 140 below.

64. *Muse.* Wonder. Cf. *K. John,* iii. 1. 317 : " I muse your majesty doth seem so cold ;" *Cor.* iii. 2. 7 :

> "I muse my mother
> Does not approve me further," etc.

See also *Macb.* p. 219.

67. *Valentinus.* The reading of the 1st folio. The later folios have "Valentino " (which Coll. claims for his MS.), and Warb. gives "Valentine."

69. *Exhibition.* Allowance ; as in *Lear,* i. 2. 25, *Oth.* i. 3. 238, iv. 3. 75, *Cymb.* i. 6. 122, etc.

84. *Resembleth.* Here a quadrisyllable. So *dazzled* is a trisyllable in ii. 4. 208 below. Gr. 477. Pope reads "resembleth well," and Johnson suggests "resembleth right," with "light " in place of *sun* in 86 for the sake of the rhyme.

ACT II.

SCENE I.—2. *One.* There is a play on *one* and *on*, which seem to have been sometimes pronounced alike ; though elsewhere we find *one* rhyming to *bone* (*V. and A.* 293), *alone* (*Sonn.* 39. 6), *Scone* (*Macb* v. 8. 74), and *thrown* (*Cymb.* v. 4. 61).

I

16. *By these special marks*, etc. Cf. *A. Y. L.* iii. 2. 392 fol.

17. *To wreathe your arms.* Cf. *L. L. L.* iv. 3. 135 : " his wreathed arms," etc.

21. *Takes diet.* Is dieting for his health.

23. *Hallowmas.* All-Hallows or All-Saints Day, November 1st, when, as Tollet says, "the poor people in Staffordshire, and perhaps in other country places, go from parish to parish *a-souling*, as they call it ; that is, begging and *puling* (or singing small, as Bailey's *Dict.* explains *puling*) for *soul-cakes*, or any good thing to make them merry."

27. *With a mistress.* By a mistress. Gr. 193. *That*=so that ; as in 35 below. Gr. 283.

30. *Without.* The play on the word needs no explanation.

33. *None else would.* " None else would be so simple " (Johnson) ; or, perhaps, as Clarke explains it, "unless you were so simple as to let your love-tokens exteriorly appear, no one would perceive them but myself."

36. *To comment on your malady.* Like the doctors who used to judge of diseases by inspecting the patient's water. See *T. N.* p. 153 (note on *Water*), or *2 Hen. IV.* p. 152 (on *What says the doctor*, etc.).

39. *She, I mean.* On *she*=her, see Gr. 211.

55. *Account of her beauty.* Appreciate her beauty.

66. *Going ungartered.* This is one of the marks of a lover in *A. Y. L.* iii. 2. See on 16 above.

70. *Put on your hose.* That is, to put them on properly. The Camb. editors believe that a rhyme was intended, and suggest "cannot see to beyond your nose " or "to put spectacles on your nose," or "to put on your shoes." H. adopts the first of these conjectures.

71. *Belike.* It is likely, probably.

74. *Swinged.* Whipped ; as in iii. 1. 369 below.

77. *Set.* Seated, as opposed to *stand*, with a play on the word.

85. *Motion.* The word meant a puppet-show, and sometimes a single puppet. Cf. *W. T.* iv. 3. 103 : "a motion of the Prodigal Son ;" and see our ed. p. 186. *Interpret* alludes to the master of the puppet-show, or the *interpreter*, as he was called, who was the speaker for the inanimate actors. Cf. *R. of L.* 1326 :

> " To see sad sights moves more than hear them told ;
> For then the eye *interprets* to the ear
> The heavy *motion* that it doth behold,
> When every part a part of woe doth bear ;"

and *Ham.* iii. 2. 256 : " I could interpret between you and your love, if I could see the puppets dallying." See *Ham.* p. 228.

88. *Give ye good even.* That is, *God* give you good even. Sometimes the verb is omitted ; as in *R. and J.* ii. 4. 115 : "God ye good morrow !" For other contractions, cf. *L. L. L.* iv. 1. 42 : "God dig-you-den !" *R. and J.* i. 2. 58 : "God gi' good-den !" ("Godgidoden" in the folio), etc.

90. *Sir Valentine and servant.* " Sir J. Hawkins says, ' Here Silvia calls her lover *servant*, and again her *gentle servant*. This was the common language of ladies to their lovers, at the time when Shakspere wrote.' Steevens gives several examples of this. Henry James Pye, in his ' Comments on the Commentators,' mentions that, ' in the *Noble Gentlemen* of

Beaumont and Fletcher, the lady's gallant has no other name in the dramatis personæ than servant,' and that 'mistress and servant are always used for lovers in Dryden's plays.' It is clear to us, however, that Shakspere here uses the words in a much more general sense than that which expresses the relations between two lovers. At the very moment that Valentine calls Silvia mistress, he says that he has written for her a letter,—'some lines to one she loves,'—unto a 'secret nameless friend;' and what is still stronger evidence that the word 'servant' had not the full meaning of lover, but meant a much more general admirer, Valentine, introducing Proteus to Silvia, says,

> 'Sweet lady, entertain him
> To be my fellow-servant to your ladyship;'

and Silvia, consenting, says to Proteus,

> 'Servant, you are welcome to a worthless mistress.'

"Now, when Silvia says this, which, according to the meaning which has been attached to the words servant and mistress, would be a speech of endearment, she had accepted Valentine really as her betrothed lover, and she had been told by Valentine that Proteus

> 'Had come along with me, but that his mistress
> Did hold his eyes lock'd in her crystal looks.'

"It appears, therefore, that we must receive these words in a very vague sense, and regard them as titles of courtesy, derived, perhaps, from the chivalric times, when many a harnessed knight and sportive troubadour described the lady whom they had gazed upon in the tilt-yard as their 'mistress,' and the same lady looked upon each of the gallant train as a 'servant' dedicated to the defence of her honour, or the praise of her beauty " (K.).

97. *Clerkly.* "Like a scholar " (Steevens) ; or, perhaps, like a good penman (Schmidt). It has the former sense in 2 *Hen. VI.* iii. 1. 179 : "With ignominious words, though clerkly couch'd " (that is, adroitly put).

102. *Stead.* Be of use to, help ; as in *Temp.* i. 2. 165, *M. of V.* i. 3. 7, etc. The folios have "steed."

111. *Quaintly.* Finely, elegantly. Cf. *M. of V.* ii. 4. 6 : "'T is vile, unless it may be quaintly order'd," etc. See also on the adjective in *Much Ado*, p. 149.

120. *So.* That is, so be it, well and good. Cf. *M. W.* iii. 4. 67 : "If it be my luck, so ; if not, happy man be his dole !"

130. *Reasoning.* Saying, talking. Cf. *M. of V.* p. 145. For the combination of *rhyme* and *reason* in Speed's reply, cf. *M. W.* v. 5. 133, *C. of E.* ii. 2. 149, *A. Y. L.* iii. 2. 418, etc.

136. *By a figure.* In the rhetorical sense.

144. *Earnest.* "Used in opposition to *jest*, and in the sense of pledge, or token of future and farther bestowal " (Clarke).

147. *And there an end.* And that is the end of it, there 's no more to say ; as in i. 3. 65 above.

153. *In print.* "With exactness" (Steevens); as if quoting the lines.

It is not necessary, however, to *print* the lines as a quotation, as some editors do ; for of course they are really Speed's own.

156. *Chameleon.* For the old notion that the chameleon lived on air, cf. *Ham.* iii. 2. 98 : "of the chameleon's dish ; I eat the air." See also ii. 4. 26 below.

159. *Be moved.* " Have compassion on me, though your mistress has none on you " (Malone).

Scene II.—4. *Turn not.* That is, are not inconstant. Cf. *Hen. V.* iii. 6. 35 : "she is turning and inconstant," etc.

5. *Keep this remembrance,* etc. Here we have an instance of the formal *betrothal* of the olden times. Cf. *T. N.* p. 160, note on *Plight me,* etc.

Scene III.—2. *Kind.* Kindred, race.

12. *Parting.* Departure. Cf. i. 1. 71 above.

13. *This left shoe.* Cf. *K. John,* p. 167, note on *Contrary feet.*

19. *I am the dog,* etc. This note of Johnson's is too good to be omitted : " This passage is much confused, and of confusion the present reading makes no end. Sir T. Hanmer reads, ' *I am the dog, no, the dog is himself,* and I am me, the dog is the dog, and I am myself.' This certainly is more reasonable, but I know not how much reason the author intended to bestow on Launce's soliloquy."

25. *Like an old woman.* The folios have "like a would woman." Theo. changed "would" to "wood" (=mad), and the Coll. MS. to " wild." Pope has "an ould woman." As W. remarks, "the words are probably written ' an ould woman,' which might be easily mistaken for ' a would woman ;' much more easily than ' wood ' for ' would.' " W. reads " O, that shoe could speak now," and takes the sentence to be, " not parenthetical, but the counterpart of the remark about that with the better sole ;" that is, " the father-shoe ' should . . . *not* speak a word,' while the mother-shoe ' *should,* or could, speak . . . like an old woman.' " But there is no need of changing *she* to " shoe," for Launce identifies the shoe with his mother. It is true that he has said *the shoe* in referring to his father just before ; but if he had said *he* there, it would have been just as natural.

26. *Up and down.* Out and out, exactly. Cf. *Much Ado,* ii. 1. 124 : " here 's his dry hand up and down," etc.

45. *In thy tail !* Hanmer reads " In my tail ?"

Scene IV.—7. The *Exit* here is due to the Camb. editors, who say : " As Speed after line 7 does not say a word during the whole of this long scene, we have sent him off the stage. It is not likely that the clown would be kept on as a mute bystander, especially when he had to appear in the following scene."

18. *Quote.* Note, mark. The word was sometimes written and pronounced *cote* ; hence the pun on *coat* in Valentine's reply. Cf. *Ham.* p. 201.

20. *My jerkin is a doublet.* K. remarks : " The *jerkin,* or jacket, was generally worn over the doublet ; but occasionally the doublet was worn

alone, and, in many instances, is confounded with the jerkin. Either had sleeves or not, as the wearer fancied; for by the inventories and wardrobe accounts of the time, we find that the sleeves were frequently separate articles of dress, and attached to the doublet, jerkin, coat, or even woman's gown, by laces or ribbands, at the pleasure of the wearer. A 'doblet jaquet' and hose of blue velvet, cut upon cloth of gold, embroidered, and a 'doblet hose and jaquet' of purple velvet, embroidered, and cut upon cloth of gold, and lined with black satin, are entries in an inventory of the wardrobe of Henry VIII.

"In 1535, a jerkin of purple velvet, with purple satin sleeves, embroidered all over with Venice gold, was presented to the king by Sir Richard Cromwell; and another jerkin of crimson velvet, with wide sleeves of the same coloured satin, is mentioned in the same inventory."

26. *Than live in your air.* See on ii. 1. 156 above.

52. *Don.* Ritson was disposed to omit this, as the characters are Italians, not Spaniards; but cf. "Don Alphonso" in i. 3. 39 above.

54. *Worth.* Changed in the Coll. MS. to "wealth;" but the repetition in *worthy* is quite in Shakespeare's manner. H. compares 72 below.

60. *Know.* The folios have "knew;" corrected by Hanmer.

61. *Convers'd.* Associated; as in i. 3. 31 above.

63. *Omitting.* Neglecting; as in *Temp.* i. 2. 183, ii. 1. 194, *J. C.* iv. 3. 229, etc.

71. *Feature.* Person, form. Cf. *Hen. VIII.* iii. 2. 50: "complete In mind and feature." See also *Ham.* p. 220.

73. *Beshrew me.* See on i. 1. 121 above.

83. *Cite.* Urge; not to be printed "'cite," as by Malone and some other editors. It is a figurative use of *cite*=summon, not a contraction of *incite.*

96. *Wink.* Shut the eyes. See on i. 2. 139 above.

97. *Exit Thurio.* As the folios give 114 below to Thurio, it is evident that he must have left the stage, though his exit is not marked in the early eds. Coll. was the first to insert it here, and is followed by W. and the Camb. ed. Theo., followed by many editors, gives 114 to a servant. D. says that "Thurio, after what the Duke, in the presence of Silvia, had said to him about welcoming Proteus, would hardly run off the moment Proteus appeared." The Camb. editors reply: "But Thurio is not held up as a model of courtesy, and he might as well be off the stage as on it, for any welcome he gives to Proteus. Besides, in 102 Valentine ignores Thurio altogether, who, if he had been present, would not have remained silent under the slight." H. thinks that Thurio's coming in to do the message "is hardly consistent with what follows,—*Come, Sir Thurio;*" but we cannot imagine why. It seems natural enough that as he has brought the message from her father she should ask him to escort her to the Duke.

102. *Entertain him.* Take him into your service. Cf. iv. 4. 56, 63, 84 below.

135. *As I confess.* That I confess. Gr. 109.

136. *To.* In comparison with; as in 164 below. Gr. 187.

137. *No such.* Changed by Hanmer to "any."

144. *An earthly paragon.* Cf. *Cymb.* iii. 6. 44:

> "By Jupiter, an angel! or, if not,
>   An earthly paragon."

149. *By her.* Of her. Cf. *M. of V.* i. 2. 60: "How say you by the French lord, Monsieur Le Bon?" Gr. 145.

150. *A principality.* Johnson explained this as = "the first or *principal* of women;" but *principality* was a term applied to one of the orders of angels, and that may be the sense here. Mason paraphrases the passage thus: "If you will not acknowledge her as divine, let her at least be considered as an angel of the first order, superior to everything on earth." Steevens cites *Romans,* viii. 38; and W. adds Milton. *P. L.* vi. 445: "Nisroc, of principalities the prime."

157. *Lest the base earth,* etc. Cf. *Rich. II.* iii. 3. 190:

> "Fair cousin, you debase your princely knee
> To make the base earth proud with kissing it;"

and *V. and A.* 721:

> "But if thou fall, O, then imagine this,—
> The earth, in love with thee, thy footing trips,
> And all is but to rob thee of a kiss."

160. *Summer-swelling.* The Coll. MS. has "summer-smelling;" and Steevens was at first inclined to that reading, but rejected it on meeting with *summer-swelling* in Gorges's *Lucan.*

164. *Worthies.* W. changes this to "worth as," on the ground that in the time of S. *worthies* "was exclusively applied to warlike heroes;" but he retains *worthies* in *L. L. L.* iv. 3. 236, where it can hardly mean "warlike heroes," either literally or figuratively:

> "Of all complexions the cull'd sovereignty
> Do meet, as at a fair, in her fair cheek,
> Where several worthies make one dignity,
> Where nothing wants that want itself doth seek."

165. *Then.* Hanmer has "Why, then."

173. *Only for.* Only because. Cf. *M. of V.* p. 134, note on *For he is a Christian.* Gr. 151.

181. *Greed.* Not "'greed," as usually printed. See Wb.

184. *Inquire you forth.* Inquire you out. Cf. "chalked forth" (*Temp.* v. 1. 203), "find forth" (*C. of E.* i. 2. 37), "point forth" (*IV. T.* iv. 4. 572), etc.

185. *Road.* Haven. See on i. 1. 53 above.

190. *Even as one heat,* etc. A proverbial expression. Cf. *J. C.* iii. 1. 171: "As fire drives out fire, so pity pity;" *R. and J.* i. 2. 46: "Tut, man, one fire burns out another's burning;" *K. John,* iii. 1. 277:

> "And falsehood falsehood cures, as fire cools fire
> Within the scorched veins of one new-burn'd;"

and *Cor.* iv. 7. 54: "One fire drives out one fire, one nail one nail."

194. *Is it mine eye,* etc. The 1st folio reads: "It is mine, or *Valentines* praise;" the later folios: "Is it mine then, or Valentineans praise?" Rowe and Pope give, "Is it mine then, or Valentino's praise;" and Theo.

" Is it mine eye, or Valentino's praise." Hanmer has the same, except
" eyne " for "eye ;" Capell, " Is it mine own, or Valentino's praise ;" and
Malone, " Is it her mien, or Valentinus' praise." *Mine eye*, as the Camb.
editors remark, is supported by *C. of E.* iii. 2. 55 : " It is a fault that
springeth from your eye." W. follows Malone ; H. reads as in the text.

199. *A waxen image.* " Alluding to the figures made by witches, as
representatives of those whom they designed to torment or destroy "
(Steevens). Cf. *K. John,* v. 4. 24 :

> "even as a form of wax
> Resolveth from his figure 'gainst the fire."

See also *Macb.* p. 133.

203. *Too too.* Some print "too-too." See *M. of V.* p. 143, note on
Too-too light.

205. *More advice.* " Further knowledge " (Steevens). Cf. *M. of V.*
iv. 2. 6, *M. for M.* v. 1. 469, etc.

207. *'T is but her picture.* Johnson, taking this literally, considered it
"evidently a slip of attention ;" but, as Steevens remarks, " Proteus
means to say that, as yet, he had seen only her outside form, without
having known her long enough to have any acquaintance with her mind."
Cf. *Cymb.* i. 6. 15 :

> "All of her that is out of door most rich I
> If she be furnish'd with a mind so rare,
> She is alone the Arabian bird."

208. *Dazzled.* A trisyllable. The later folios add "so." See on *resembleth,* i. 3. 84 above.

The meaning of the passage is : " Her mere outside has *dazzled* me ;
when I am acquainted with the perfections of her mind, I shall be struck
blind " (Malone).

SCENE V.—1. *Milan.* The folios have " Padua," as " Verona " in iii.
1. 81 and v. 4. 129. The Camb. editors believe that S. wrote the whole
of the play before he had finally determined where the scene·was to be
laid. Halliwell suggests that " Padua " is perhaps a relic of some old
Italian story, upon which the play may have been founded.

5. *Shot.* Cf. Falstaff's play upon the word in 1 *Hen. IV.* v. 3. 31 :
"'Though I could scape shot-free at London, I fear the shot here."

16. *Are they broken ?* Have they broken, or fallen out?

22. *My staff understands me.* Johnson notes that Milton has used the
same quibble in *P. L.* vi. 625 :

> "To whom thus Belial, in like gamesome mood :
> Leader, the terms we sent were terms of weight,
> Of hard contents, and full of force urg'd home ;
> Such as we might perceive amus'd them all,
> And stumbled many: who receives them right
> Had need from head to foot well understand ;
> Not understood, this gift they had besides,
> They show us when our foes walk not upright."

35. *How sayest thou, that my master,* etc. " What sayest thou to this
circumstance,—namely, that my master, etc." (Malone). Cf. *Macb.* p. 222,
note on *How say'st thou,* etc.

44. *If thou wilt*, etc. In the folios there is no comma after *wilt*, and the 2d folio has "If thou wilt go with me to the alehouse, so." The pointing in the text is due to K.

49. *Go to the ale.* Launce plays upon *ale* as applied to a church-ale, or rural festival. Cf. *Per.* prol. 6: "On ember-eves and holy-ales."

SCENE VI.—1, 2. The folios have "forsworn?" in both lines. Theo. was the first to change the pointing. For the "indefinite use" of the infinitive in these lines, see Gr. 356. Cf. iii. 1. 185 below.

7. *Sweet-suggesting.* Sweetly tempting, seductive. For *suggest* = tempt, cf. iii. 1. 34 below. Warb. changed *If thou hast sinn'd* to "If I have sinn'd;" but the preceding line shows what is meant.

13. *Learn.* Teach; as in *Temp.* i. 2. 365; "learning me your language," etc. Cf. v. 3. 4 below.

17. *Leave to love.* Cf. iii. 1. 182 below: "leave to be," etc.

35. *Competitor.* Confederate, partner. Cf. *L. L. L.* ii. 1. 82: "he and his competitors in oath," etc. See also *T. N.* p. 158.

37. *Pretended.* Johnson conjectured "intended;" but *pretend* is sometimes = intend. Cf. *R. of L.* 576:

> * Quoth she, 'Reward not hospitality
> With such black payment as thou hast pretended;'"

Macb. ii. 4. 24: "What good could they pretend?" etc. So *pretence* = intention; as in *IV. T.* iii. 2. 18, *Cor.* i. 2. 20, etc. See also iii. 1. 47 below.

41. *Blunt.* Dull in understanding; as in 2 *Hen. IV.* ind. 18: "the blunt monster with uncounted heads," etc.

SCENE VII.—2. *Conjure.* Accented by S. on either syllable, without regard to the meaning. See *M. N. D.* p. 164.

3. *Table.* Tablet; the "table-book" of *IV. T.* iv. 4. 610 and *Ham.* ii. 2. 136. Cf. *Ham.* i. 5. 98: "the table of my memory," etc.

4. *Character'd.* Written. Cf. *Sonn.* 108. 1: "What 's in the brain that ink may character," etc. For the accent, cf. *R. of L.* 807: "The light will show, character'd in my brow," etc. Gr. 490.

5. *Mean.* For the singular, cf. iii. 1. 38 and iv. 4. 101 below. See also *R. and J.* p. 189.

9. *A true-devoted pilgrim*, etc. K. remarks: "The comparison which Julia makes between the ardour of her passion and the enthusiasm of the pilgrim is exceedingly beautiful. When travelling was a business of considerable danger and personal suffering, the pilgrim, who was not weary

> 'To traverse kingdoms with his feeble steps,'

to encounter the perils of a journey to Rome, or Loretto, or Compostella, or Jerusalem, was a person not to be looked upon as thoroughly in earnest.

"In the time of Shakspere the pilgrimages to the tomb of St. Thomas à Becket, at Canterbury, which Chaucer has rendered immortal, were discontinued; and few, perhaps, undertook the sea voyage to Jerusalem. But the pilgrimage to the shrine of St. James, or St. Jago, the patron-saint of Spain, at Compostella, was undertaken by all classes of Catholics. The House of Our Lady at Loretto was, however, the great object of the devotee's vows; and, at particular seasons, there were not fewer than two hundred thousand pilgrims visiting it at once. The Holy House (the *Santa Casa*) is the house in which the Blessed Virgin is said to have been born, in which she was betrothed to Joseph, and where the annunciation of the Angel was made. It is pretended that it was carried, on the 9th of May, 1291, by supernatural means, from Galilee to Tersato, in Dalmatia; and from thence removed, on the 10th of December, 1294, to Italy, where it was deposited in a wood at midnight. The Santa Casa (which now stands within the large church of Loretto) consists of one room, the length of which is 31¾ feet, the breadth 13 feet, and the height 18 feet. On the ceiling is painted the Assumption of the Virgin Mary; and other paintings once adorned the walls of the apartment. On the west side is the window through which the Angel is said to have entered the house; and facing it, in a niche, is the image of the Virgin and Child, which was once enriched by the offerings of princes and devotees. The mantle, or robe, which she had on was covered with innumerable jewels of inestimable value, and she had a triple crown of gold enriched with pearls and diamonds, given her by Louis XIII. of France. The niche in which the figure stands was adorned with seventy-one large Bohemian topazes, and on the right side of the image is an angel of cast gold, profusely enriched with diamonds and other gems. A great part of these treasures was taken by Pope Pius VII., in order to pay to France the sum extorted by the treaty of Tolentino, in 1797. They have been partially replaced since by new contributors, among whom have been Murat, Eugène Beauharnais, and other members of the Bonaparte family. There are a few relics considered more valuable than the richest jewels that have been carried away. Notwithstanding the mean appearance of the walls within the Santa Casa, the outside is encased, and adorned with the finest Carrara marble. The work was begun in 1514, in the pontificate of Leo X., and the House of Our Lady was consecrated in 1538. The expense of this casing amounted to 50,000 crowns, and the most celebrated sculptors of the age were employed. Bramante was the architect, and Baccio Bandinelli assisted in the sculptures. The whole was completed in 1579, in the pontificate of Gregory XIII. The munificent expenditure upon the House of Our Lady at Loretto, had, probably, contributed greatly to make the pilgrimage the most attractive in Europe, when Shakspere wrote."

18. *Inly*. Again used as an adjective in 3 *Hen. VI.* i. 4. 171: "inly sorrow." We find it as an adverb in *Temp.* v. 1. 200 and *Hen. V.* iv. chor. 24.

Clarke remarks here: "S. uses the word *touch* with varied and powerful meaning. Here—joined with *inly* for inward, or rather innermost—it conveys the idea of that fine and subtle feeling which penetrates to the heart's core."

22. *Fire's*. A dissyllable; as in i. 2. 30 above. *Extreme* is accented on the first syllable by S. except in *Sonn.* 129. 4, 10. The superlative is always *extrémest*.

32. *Ocean*. A trisyllable; as in Milton, *Hymn on Nativity*, 66: " Whis-

pering new joys to the mild ocean." Gr. 479. The Coll. MS. changes *wild* to "wide."

42. *Weeds.* Garments. Cf. *M. N. D.* ii. 2. 71: "Weeds of Athens he doth wear," etc. So also the singular; as in *M. N. D.* ii. 1. 256, *Cor.* ii. 3. 229, etc.

51. *Farthingale.* A hoop petticoat. Cf. *M. IV.* iii. 3. 69: "a semi-circled farthingale." In *T. of S.* iv. 3. 56 we find "fardingales."

53. *Codpiece.* A portion of the male attire, made indelicately conspicuous in the time of S. Cf. *L. L. L.* iii. 1. 186, *M. for M.* iii. 2. 122, etc. Malone remarks that allusions to it, even in the mouth of a lady, were not considered indecorous in that day.

70. *Instances of infinite of love.* The reading of the 1st folio; the 2d has "as infinite." Malone reads "of the infinite," which is favoured by "the infinite of thought" in *Much Ado,* ii. 3. 106; but, as W. remarks, the text is sustained by other passages in old writers. *Infinite* of course = infinity.

85. *Longing.* Changed in the Coll. MS. to "loving." "But," as Clarke asks, "could there be a more Shakespearianly comprehensive word here than *longing?* Julia, who has just talked of having 'pined,' 'longing' for the sight of Proteus, now speaks of the journey that she longs to take, that she longs to reach the end of, and longingly hopes to crown by beholding him."

86. *Dispose.* For the noun, cf. iv. 1. 76 below. See also *C. of E.* i. 1. 21, *K. John,* i. 1. 263, etc.

87. *Reputation.* Metrically five syllables. See on 32 above.

90. *Turriance.* We find the word again in *P. P.* 74: "a longing tarriance."

ACT III.

SCENE I.—1. *Give us leave.* A courteous form of dismissal. Cf. *M. IV.* ii. 2. 165: "Give us leave, drawer;" *K. John,* i. 1. 230: "James Gurney, wilt thou give us leave awhile?" etc.

21. *Timeless.* Untimely; the only meaning in S. except perhaps in *R. of L.* 44. Cf. *R and J.* p. 217. Pope changes *Being* to "If."

28. *Aim.* Guess, conjecture. Cf. *J. C.* i. 2. 163: "What you would work me to, I have some aim," etc. Cf. also the verb in 45 below, and in *T. of S.* ii. 1. 237, *R. and J.* i. 1. 211, etc.

34. *Suggested.* Tempted. See on ii. 6. 7 above.

38. *Mean.* See on ii. 7. 5 above.

47. *Publisher.* One who exposes or brings to light; as in *R. of L.* 33, the only other instance of the word in S.

For *pretence* = intention, see on ii. 6. 37 above. Johnson makes *pretence* = "claim made to your daughter."

59. *Break with thee.* See on i. 3. 44 above.

65. *Full of virtue,* etc. "The way in which Valentine here belies his own dignity as a gentleman, and compromises that of his mistress as a lady worthy all excellence in the match she should make, by speaking

thus untruly of the husband proposed, affords one of the many evidences that this play was one of Shakespeare's earliest compositions" (Clarke).

68. *Peevish.* Foolishly or childishly wayward ; as in *T. of S.* v. 2. 157 : "she is peevish, froward, sullen, sour," etc. Cf. *Hen. V.* p. 171.

73. *Upon advice.* On reflection, or consideration. Cf. ii. 4. 205 above. See also *M. of V.* p. 161.

74. *Where.* Whereas ; as in *M. of V.* iv. 1. 22, *Rich. II.* iii. 2. 185, 1 *Hen. IV.* iv. 1. 53, etc. Gr. 134.

81. *Of Verona.* The folios have "in Verona," and "Verona" in v. 4. 129 below, where, as here, we should expect *Milan.* Pope reads "sir, in Milan," and the Coll. MS. "in Milano." *Of Verona* is Halliwell's emendation, adopted by W. and others. W. suggests that "the Duke made his pretended mistress a Veronese, the better to justify his application to her townsman for advice." See on ii. 5. 1 above.

84. *To my tutor.* For *to* = for, see *Temp.* p. 124 (note on *A paragon to their queen*), or Gr. 189.

85. *Agone.* An earlier form of *ago,* used by S. only here.

87. *Bestow myself.* Deport myself ; but only reflexively in this sense. Cf. 2 *Hen. IV.* ii. 2. 186 : "How might we see Falstaff bestow himself to-night in his true colours, and not ourselves be seen ?" See also *A. Y. L.* iv. 3. 87, *K. John,* iii. 1. 225, etc.

88. *Sun-bright.* Cf. *silver-bright* in *K. John,* ii. 1. 315.

89. *Respect not.* Regard not, take no notice of. Cf. i. 2. 134 above, and iv. 4. 174, v. 4. 20, 54 below.

93. *Contents.* Pleases, gratifies ; as often in S. Cf. *T. of S.* iv. 3. 180, *W. T.* ii. 1. 159, *Ham.* iii. 1. 24, etc. For the noun (=happiness, joy), see *Oth.* p. 174.

99. *For why.* W. prints "For why !—the fools," etc., and the Camb. ed. and others, "For why, the fools," etc. H. says that both are "evidently wrong," and that there should be no point after *why,* as *for why* = because. There is no doubt that *for why* in some instances (cf. *Rich. II.* p. 208 and *C. of E.* p. 129) became practically =because, or, as Abbott gives it (Gr. 75), "wherefore ? (because) ;" but this is merely a modification of the ordinary interrogative construction, and the comma may well be used to distinguish it from the regular use of *for* and *for that* =because (Gr. 151).

109. *That.* So that ; as in 112 and 129 below. See also on ii. 1. 27 above.

113. *Lets.* Hinders ; as in *Ham.* i. 4. 85 : "I 'll make a ghost of him that lets me," etc. Cf. *Exod.* v. 4, *Isa.* xliii. 13, *Rom.* i. 13, etc. For the noun (=hindrance), see *Hen. V.* p. 185.

116. *Apparent.* Evident, manifest. Cf. *M. for M.* iv. 2. 144 :

> "*Duke.* It is now apparent?
> *Provost.* Most manifest, and not denied by himself."

See also *Rich. II.* p. 150, or *J. C.* p. 147.

117. *Quaintly.* Deftly, skilfully. See on ii. 1. 111 above.

120. *Adventure.* Venture. Cf. *W. T.* i. 2. 38: "I 'll adventure The borrow of a week ;" *Id.* ii. 3. 162 :

"what will you adventure
To save this brat's life?" etc.

138. *Engine.* Used by S. for any instrument or device. Cf. *V. and A.*
367: "the engine of her thoughts" (her tongue); *A. IV.* iii. 5. 21: "prom-
ises, enticements, oaths, tokens, and all these engines of lust;" *Oth.* iii.
3. 355: "mortal engines" (cannon), etc.

144. *In thy pure bosom.* Cf. 250 below. In the poet's time ladies had
a small pocket in the front of their stays, in which they carried letters,
love-tokens, etc. Cf. *Ham.* ii. 2. 113: "In her excellent white bosom,
these," etc. Malone quotes one of Lord Surrey's *Sonnets,* in which he
says to the "song" he sends his mistress: "Between her brests she
shall thee put, there shall she thee reserve."

145. *Importune.* For the accent, see on i. 3. 13 above.

148. *For.* Because. See on 99 and ii. 4. 173 above.

153. *Why, Phaethon,* etc. "Thou art Phaethon in thy rashness, but
without his pretensions; thou art not the son of a divinity, but a *terra*
filius, a low-born wretch: Merops is thy true father, with whom Phaethon
was falsely reproached" (Johnson). It will be remembered that in the
old fable, Phaethon was the son of Phœbus by Clymene, the wife of
Merops.

154. *Car.* Both the 3d and the 4th folio misprint "cat."

156. *Wilt thou reach stars,* etc. Coll. notes that, in Greene's *Pandosto*
(on which *W. T.* is founded), Fawnia exclaims, in reference to her love
for the prince, "Stars are to be looked at with the eye, not reached at
with the hand."

182. *Leave to be.* Cf. ii. 6. 17 above.

185. *To fly.* In flying. See on ii. 6. 1 above. The folios have "his"
for *this,* which is due to D. Sr. conjectures "is deadly doom."

189. *So ho, so ho!* The cry of the hunter on starting a hare. Cf. *R.*
and J. ii. 4. 136. This will explain the play on *hair* in Launce's next
speech.

200. *Who wouldst thou strike?* Cf. *Cor.* ii. 1. 8: "Who does the wolf
love?" Gr. 274. The 2d folio has "Whom."

234. *Repeal.* Recall. See *J. C.* p. 157, note on *The repealing of my*
banish'd brother. Cf. the verb in v. 4. 143 below.

247. *Manage.* Handle, wield; often used of implements or weapons.
Cf. *Rich. II.* iii. 2. 118, 2 *Hen. IV.* iii. 2. 292, 301, *R. and J.* i. 1. 76, etc.

263. *But one knave.* This probably means a *single* knave, and not a
double one (cf. *Cymb.* iv. 2. 88: "thou double villain!" and *Oth.* i. 3. 400:
"double knavery"), as Johnson, Farmer, W., and others explain it. Capell paraphrases the passage thus: "My master is a kind of knave; but
that were no great matter, if he were but *one* knave; but he is *two*—a
knave to his friend, and a knave to his mistress." Clarke thinks the
meaning may possibly be "a single knave, that is, an unmarried one;"
to make his friend's intended wife his own would crown his knavery.
Hanmer reads "one kind of knave," Warb. "one kind," and H. "one
in love" (the conjecture of St.).

267. *She hath had gossips.* "*Gossips* not only signify those who answer
for a child in baptism, but the tattling women who attend lyings-in. The

quibble between these is evident" (Steevens). Cf. *Hen. VIII.* p. 205, note on *Gossip.*

270. *Bare.* "The word has two senses; *mere* and *naked.* Launce uses it in both, and opposes the *naked* female to the water-spaniel *covered with hair*" (Steevens).

Cate-log. Launce's blunder for *catalogue.* For *condition* the 4th folio and some modern eds. have "conditions."

273. *Jade.* Launce plays upon the word as applied to a worthless or vicious horse.

278. *Master's ship.* The folios have "Mastership;" corrected by Theo.

285. *Jolt-head.* Blockhead. Cf. *T. of S.* iv. 1. 169: "You heedless jolt-heads and unmanner'd slaves!"

292. *Saint Nicholas be thy speed!* Saint Nicholas help thee! Cf. *A. Y. L.* i. 2. 222: "Hercules be thy speed!" etc. K. remarks: "When Speed is about to read Launce's paper, Launce, who has previously said, 'Thou canst not read,' invokes Saint Nicholas to assist him. Saint Nicholas was the patron-saint of scholars. There is a story in Douce how the saint attained this distinction, by discovering that a wicked host had murdered three scholars on their way to school, and by his prayers restored their souls to their bodies. This legend is told in the Life of Saint Nicholas, composed in French verse by *Maitre Wace*, chaplain to Henry II., and which remains in manuscript. By the statutes of St. Paul's School, the scholars are required to attend divine service at the cathedral on the anniversary of this saint. The parish clerks of London were incorporated into a guild, with Saint Nicholas for their patron. These worthy persons were, probably, at the period of their incorporation, more worthy of the name of *clerks* (scholars) than we have been wont in modern times to consider. But why are thieves called Saint Nicholas' clerks in *Henry IV.?* Warburton says, by a quibble between Nicholas and old Nick. This we doubt. Scholars appear, from the ancient statutes against vagrancy, to have been great travellers about the country. These statutes generally recognize the right of poor scholars to beg; but they were also liable to the penalties of the gaol and the stocks, unless they could produce letters testimonial from the chancellor of their respective universities. It is not unlikely that in the journeys of these hundreds of poor scholars they should have occasionally 'taken a purse' as well as begged 'an almesse,' and that some of 'Saint Nicholas's clerks' should have become as celebrated for the same accomplishments which distinguished Bardolph and Peto at Gadshill, as for the learned poverty which entitled them to travel with a chancellor's license."

302. *Stock.* For the sense (stocking) on which Launce plays, see *T. N.* p. 126.

307. *Set the world on wheels.* This was a proverbial expression. Cf. *A. and C.* ii. 7. 99:

> "*Enobarbus.* A' bears the third part of the world, man; see'st not?
> *Menas.* The third part, then, is drunk; would it were all,
> That it might go on wheels."

See our ed. p. 190.

312. *Here follow her vices.* Some take this to be Speed's comment, not a part of the paper.

314. *Kissed.* Omitted in the folios; supplied by Rowe. W. adheres to the old text.

318. *A sweet mouth.* "What is now vulgarly called *a sweet tooth*, a luxurious desire of dainties and sweetmeats" (Johnson). Launce pretends to understand it as a compliment to her beauty.

321. *Sleep not in her talk.* The Coll. MS. changes *sleep* to "slip."

332. *Curst.* Shrewish. Cf. *T. of S.* i. 1. 185: "Her eldest sister is so curst and shrewd;" *Id.* i. 2. 128: "Katherine the curst," etc. See also *M. N. D.* p. 167.

334. *She will often praise her liquor.* "That is, show how well she likes it by drinking often" (Johnson).

337. *Liberal.* That is, too free, or wanton. Cf. *Much Ado,* p. 154, or *Ham.* p. 258.

342. *More hair than wit.* An old proverb, found in Ray's Collection. Steevens quotes Dekker, *Satiromastix:*

> "Hair ! 't is the basest stubble ; in scorn of it
> This proverb sprung,—He has more hair than wit."

349. *The cover of the salt.* "The ancient English salt-cellar was very different from the modern, being a large piece of plate generally much ornamented, with a cover, to keep the salt clean. There was but one salt-cellar on the dinner-table, which was placed near the top of the table ; and those who sat below the salt were, for the most part, of an inferior condition to those who sat above it " (Malone).

369. *Swinged.* Whipped. Cf. ii. 1. 74 above.

SCENE II.—**3.** *Exile.* S. accents both noun and verb on either syllable, according to the measure.

5. *That.* So that. See on ii. 1. 27 and iii. 1. 109 above.

6. *Impress.* Regularly accented on the last syllable by S.

7. *Trenched.* Cut. Cf. *Macb.* iii. 4. 27: "trenched gashes ;" and *V. and A.* 1052:

> "the wide wound that the boar had trench'd
> In his soft flank."

Hour's is a dissyllable. Cf. *fire* in i. 2. 30 above.

8. *His.* Its. Gr. 228.

14. *Grievously.* According to Malone, some copies of the 1st folio have "heavily," which is the reading of the later folios.

17. *Conceit.* Conception, opinion. Cf. *Hen. VIII.* ii. 3. 74 :

> "I shall not fail t' approve the fair conceit
> The king hath of you," etc.

28. *Persevers.* The only form of the verb in the folios. The quartos have " persevere " in *Lear,* iii. 5. 23. We find the word rhyming with *ever* in *A. W.* iv. 2. 36, 37. So *perseverance* is accented on the second syllable. Gr. 492.

36. *With circumstance.* "With the addition of such incidental particulars as may induce belief" (Johnson). Cf. *C. of E.* v. 1. 16: "With circumstance and oaths ;" and *K. and J.* v. 3. 181:

> "But the true ground of all these piteous woes
> We cannot without circumstance descry"

(that is, without further particulars).

41. *His very friend.* Cf. *M. of V.* iii. 2. 226: "my very friends," etc.

49. *Weed.* Rowe reads "wean."

53. *Bottom it.* Wind it. Cf. the noun *bottom* (= ball of thread) in *T. of S.* iv. 3. 138: "a bottom of brown thread." See our ed. p. 164. Steevens quotes John Grange's *Garden*, 1557:

> "A bottome for your silke it seems
> My letters are become,
> Which oft with winding off and on
> Are wasted whole and some."

64. *Where.* The Coll. MS. has "When."

68. *Lime.* That is, bird-lime. Cf. *Macb.* p. 236.

76. *Moist.* For the verb, cf. *A. and C.* v. 2. 285: "The juice of Egypt's grape shall moist this lip."

77. *Such integrity.* Malone suspected that a line had been lost after this; but, as Steevens remarks, the meaning may be "such ardour and sincerity as would be manifested by practising the directions given in the four preceding lines."

84. *Consort.* The folio reading, changed by Hanmer and most of the modern editors to "concert," a word not found in the folio. Cf. *2 Hen. VI.* iii. 2. 327: "And boding screech-owls make the consort full" ("concert" in most modern eds.). With the accent on the last syllable *consort* meant a company (as in iv. 1. 64 below); with the accent on the first syllable, a band of musicians. Cf. *R. and J.* iii. 1. 48:

> "*Tybalt.* Mercutio, thou consort'st with Romeo.
> *Mercutio.* Consort! what, dost thou make us minstrels? an thou make minstrels of us, look to hear nothing but discords;"

where Mercutio evidently plays upon *consort* = band of *minstrels*. Milton, who never uses *concert*, has *consort* repeatedly in the sense of choir or musical band; as in the *Ode at a Solemn Music*, 27:

> "O may we soon again renew that song,
> And keep in tune with Heaven, till God ere long
> To his celestial consort us unite.
> To live with him, and sing in endless morn of light!"

Hymn on Nativity, 130:

> "And, with your ninefold harmony,
> Make up full consort to the angelic symphony;"

and *Il Pens.* 145:

> "And the waters murmuring,
> With such consort as they keep,
> Entice the dewy-feather'd sleep."

Cf. also B. and F., *Captain*, I. 3:

> "Or be of some good consort;
> You had a pleasant touch of the cittern once;"

and *Night-Walker*, iii. 3:

"And tune our instrument till the consort comes
To make up the full noise"

(where *noise*=band of musicians, as in 2 *Hen. IV.* ii. 4. 13, etc.).

85. *Dump.* "A mournful elegy" (Steevens). See *Much Ado*, p. 137.

86. *Grievance.* Grief; as in *Sonn.* 30. 9, *L. C.* 67, *R. and J.* i. 1. 163, etc. So *grief* sometimes =grievance; as in v. 4. 142 below. See also 1 *Hen. IV.* p. 192.

87. *Inherit her.* Win her, gain possession of her. Cf. *R. and J.* i. 2. 30:

"even such delight
Among fresh female buds shall you to-night
Inherit at my house."

See also *Temp.* iv. 1. 154, *Rich. II.* ii. 1. 83, *Cymb.* iii. 2. 63, etc.

92. *Sort.* Sort out, select. Cf. *R. and J.* iv. 2. 34:

"To help me sort such needful ornaments
As you think fit to furnish me to-morrow."

94. *Onset.* Beginning.

98. *Pardon you.* "Excuse you from waiting" (Johnson), or your attendance upon me.

ACT IV.

SCENE I.—*A Forest near Milan.* Most of the editors place the scene "near Mantua" or "on the frontiers of Mantua" (so also v. 3 and v. 4); but we are satisfied that W. is right in placing it near Milan, though he is probably wrong in assuming that the serenade in iv. 2 is the one proposed in iii. 2 (cf. Mr. Daniel's "time-analysis," p. 154 below). The forest, however, as he says, is evidently the one which Sir Eglamour tells Silvia (v. 1. 11) is "not three leagues off" from Milan. Coll. places the scene "between Milan and Verona;" but we do not understand what W. means by saying that he (Coll.) forgets that "the road from Milan to Verona lay through Mantua." That would not be the direct route.

1. *Passenger.* Passer-by, wayfarer; as in v. 4. 15 below.

10. *Proper.* Comely. Cf. *M. of V.* p. 132, note on *A proper man's picture.*

33. *Have you the tongues?* Can you speak foreign languages? Cf. *Much Ado*, v. 1. 167: "'Nay,' said I, 'he hath the tongues.'"

35. *Often had been.* The 1st folio repeats *often* after *been;* corrected in the 2d. Coll. reads "had been often."

36. *Robin Hood's fat friar.* "The jolly Friar Tuck, of the old Robin Hood ballads—the almost equally famous Friar Tuck of *Ivanhoe*—is the personage whom the outlaws here invoke. It is unnecessary to enter upon the legends—

'Of Tuck, the merry friar, who many a sermon made,
In praise of Robin Hood, his outlaws, and his trade.'

"Shakespeare has two other allusions to Robin Hood. The old duke, in *As You Like It,* 'is already in the forest of Arden, and many merry

men with him, and there they live, like the old Robin Hood of England.'
Master Silence, that 'merry heart,' that 'man of mettle,' sings, 'in the
sweet of the night,' of—
> 'Robin Hood, Scarlet, and John.'

The honourable conditions of Robin's lawless rule over his followers
were evidently in our poet's mind when he makes Valentine say—
> 'I take your offer, and will live with you;
> Provided that you do no outrages
> On silly women, or poor passengers.' "

46. *Awful.* "Full of awe and respect for the laws of society and the
duties of life" (Malone). Schmidt compares *Per.* ii. prol. 4:
> "A better prince and benign lord,
> That will prove awful both in deed and word."

See also *Rich. II.* iii. 3. 76:
> "how dare thy joints forget
> To pay their awful duty to our presence?"

The word, however, seems a strange one here, and there is much plausi-
bility in Heath's conjecture of "lawful," which is approved by Sir J.
Hawkins, Steevens, and others. Johnson explained *awful* as "reverend,
worshipful, such as magistrates, and other principal members of civil
communities."

48. *Practising.* Plotting; as often. Cf. *A. Y. L.* p. 140. For *practice*
=plotting, trickery, see *Much Ado*, p. 156, or *Ham.* p. 255.

49. *An heir, and near allied.* The 1st and 2d folios have "And heire
and Neece, allide;" the 3d folio "An heir, and Neice allide." Theo.
made the correction, which has been adopted by the editors generally.

51. *Mood.* Rage, wrath. Cf. *C. of E.* ii. 2. 172: "Abetting him to
thwart me in my mood." See also *A. W.* v. 2. 5, *Oth.* ii. 3. 274, etc.

58. *Quality.* Profession, vocation. Cf. *Hen. V.* iii. 6. 146: "What is
thy name? I know thy quality," etc.

64. *Consort.* See on iii. 2. 84 above.

72. *Silly.* Often used as a term of pity =poor, harmless, helpless. Cf.
Rich. II. v. 5. 25: "silly beggars;" *V.* and *A.* 1098: "the silly lamb,"
etc. As Trench remarks (*Select Glossary*, s. v.), the word (identical with
the German *selig*) "has successively meant (1) blessed, (2) innocent, (3)
harmless, (4) weakly foolish."

74. *Crews.* All the early eds. have "crewes" or "crews," for which
the Coll. MS. substituted "cave" and Sr. "caves." The emendation is
plausible, and derives some little support from the next line, and perhaps
also from v. 3. 12 below; but no change seems really called for. As K.
remarks, "it was not necessary that all the outlaws should be on the
stage, leaving the treasure unguarded." W. retains *crews*, H. has "cave."
Delius conjectures "crew."

76. *Dispose.* See on ii. 7. 86 above.

SCENE II.—1. *Have I.* Pope reads "I 've."

12. *Sudden quips.* Sharp taunts or sarcasms. Cf. *Much Ado*, ii. 3.
249: "Shall quips and sentences and these paper bullets of the brain
awe a man from the career of his humour?"

K

20. *Will creep in service*, etc.   Reed notes that "Kindness will creep where it cannot gang" is found in Kelly's *Scottish Proverbs*.

Clarke remarks here : "It is curious to note how, in slight touches, in mere passing words, as in broad painting, the poet contrives to fill up and keep perpetually before us the distinctive marks of his characters. In that little monosyllable *crept* here introduced—no less than by the preceding soliloquy and the more manifest passages throughout the play—the essential meanness that characterizes Proteus is delineated. Through the impression produced upon other persons in the drama, S. often thus subtly conveys the impression he desires to produce on his audience ; and in Thurio's expression *crept* we seem to see Proteus as even the obtuse Thurio instinctively sees him,—a cringing, stealthy-stepped, base-souled man."

23. *Who?* The later folios have "Whom?" See on iii. 1. 200 above.

26. *Allicholly.* Cf. *M. W.* i. 4. 164 (Mrs. Quickly's speech) : "given too much to allicholly." Pope makes it "melancholy."

41. *The heaven such grace did lend her.* Douce cites *Per.* prol. 24 : "As heaven had lent her all his grace."

44. *Beauty lives with kindness.* "Beauty without kindness *dies* unenjoyed and undelighting" (Johnson).

54. *Likes.* Pleases. Cf. *Ham.* v. 2. 276: "This likes me well," etc. So impersonally ; as in *M. for M.* ii. 1. 33 : "if it like your honour," etc.

70. *Talk on.* For *on* = of, see Gr. 181.

73. *Out of all nick.* Beyond all reckoning ; alluding to the keeping of accounts by *nicks*, or notches, on a stick, or wooden tally. Here the expression is in keeping with the character, as inn-keepers used these tallies. Steevens quotes *A Woman Never Vexed*, 1532 :

> " I have carried
> The tallies at my girdle seven years together,
> For I did ever love to deal honestly in the nick."

80. *St. Gregory's well.* The only mention in S. of the holy wells which were the resort of pilgrims in the olden time. The town of Holywell in North Wales takes its name from the famous well of Saint Winifred, which was enclosed in a beautiful Gothic temple, erected by the mother of Henry VII. and still standing.

92. *Conceitless.* Void of understanding, stupid. For *conceit* = intellect, understanding, cf. 2 *Hen. IV.* ii. 4. 263 : "his wit 's as thick as Tewksbury mustard ; there 's no more conceit in him than is in a mallet," etc.

93. *To be seduced.* For the ellipsis of *us*, see Gr. 281.

103. *Buried.* A trisyllable. Gr. 474.

107. *Importunacy.* Accented on third syllable ; as in *T. of A.* ii. 2. 42 : "Your importunacy cease till after dinner." S. uses the word only twice.

109. *His grave.* The first folio has "her" for *his* ; corrected in the 2d.

113. *Sepulchre.* Accented on second syllable. Cf. *Lear*, p. 210.

131. *By my halidom.* By my faith as a Christian. See Wb. s. v. S. uses the phrase only here. Cf. Spenser, *Mother Hubberds Tale*, 545 : "Now sure, and by my hallidome, (quoth he)," etc.

132. *Lies.* Lodges. Cf. 2 *Hen. IV.* iii. 2. 299: "when I lay at Clement's Inn ;" and see our ed. pp. 179, 185.

136. *Most heaviest.* For double comparatives and superlatives in S., see Gr. 11.

SCENE III.—D. and H. make this scene and the next a continuation of the preceding. The latter remarks: "As there is confessedly no change of place, but only of persons, there is plainly no cause for marking a new scene." But there *is* a change of *time*—to the next day, in fact—which is surely a sufficient reason for a new scene. The preceding scene is at night, and Julia has just denied that it is "almost day;" the present scene is early the next morning, but we must assume an interval of at least several hours. Scene iv. is evidently later in the day when Launce is returning from Silvia with his dog which she has refused to accept. In the meantime Julia in disguise has entered the service of Proteus, and he now sends her to Silvia to claim the picture the latter had promised him *the night before.* It is absurd to crowd into a single scene all these events distributed through a night and the following day, and separated by other events occurring off the stage but essential to the plot.

9. *Impose.* Injunction, command; the only instance of the noun in S. Cf. *dispose* in ii. 7. 86 and iv. 1. 76 above.

14. *Valiant, wise,* etc. The verse limps, and Pope reads "Valiant and wise," etc. "Wise, valiant" has been suggested, making *valiant* a trisyllable (Gr. 479), which it could not well be at the beginning of the line.

Remorseful. Pitiful, compassionate; the only meaning in S. Cf. *Rich. III.* p. 185; and for *remorse*=pity, *Id.* p. 221, or *Macb.* p. 171.

17. *Enforce me marry.* Force me to marry. For the ellipsis of *to,* see Gr. 349.

18. *Abhors.* The folios have "abhor'd" or "abhorr'd;" corrected by Hanmer.

22. *Thou vow'dst pure chastity.* It was common in former ages for widowers and widows to make vows of chastity in honour of their deceased wives or husbands; and this seems sometimes to have been done as a tribute to one merely betrothed, which was probably Sir Eglamour's case.

25. *And for.* And because. See on ii. 4. 173 above.

32. *Rewards.* Changed by Pope to "reward;" but the singular verb is often found with two singular subjects. Cf. v. 4. 73 below. See also Gr. 336.

38. *Grievances.* Explained by Johnson as = "sorrows, sorrowful affections." The word sometimes had this sense (as in iii. 2. 86 above), but here, as Clarke remarks, "the enforced marriage with a man whom her soul abhors, the most unholy match from which she would fly, seem to give support to the word being taken in its usual meaning of injuries menaced or inflicted, grounds for complaint."

The Coll. MS. adds here (after 38) the line, "And the most true affections that you bear." As W. says, this is not only unnecessary and wanton, but it makes Sir Eglamour pity Silvia's *affections* as well as her grievances, though he admits that they are "virtuously placed."

41. *Recking.* Caring. The folios have "Wreaking;" as in some other passages. So *reckless* sometimes appears as "wreakless."

42. *Befortune.* Betide; used by S. only here.

SCENE IV.—*Enter* LAUNCE *with his Dog.* The poet Campbell asks :
" What shall we say to Launce and his dog ? Is it probable that even
such a fool as Launce should have put his feet into the stocks for the
puddings which his dog had stolen, or poked his head through the pillory
for the murder of geese which the same dog had killed ?—yet the ungrate-
ful cur never denies one item of the facts with which Launce so tenderly
reproaches him. Nay, what is more wonderful, this enormous outrage
on the probable excites our common risibility. What an unconscionable
empire over our fanciful faith is assumed by those comic geniuses ! They
despise the very word probability. Only think of Smollett making us laugh
at the unlikely speech of Pipes, spoken to Commodore Trunnion down a
chimney—' Commodore Trunnion, get up and be spliced, or lie still and be
damned !' And think also of Swift amusing us with contrasted descrip-
tions of men six inches and sixty feet high—how very improbable !'
    " At the same time, something may be urged on the opposite side of
the question. A fastidious sense of the improbable would be sometimes
a nuisance in comic fiction. One sees dramatic critics often trying the
probabilities of incidents in a play, as if they were testing the evidence
of facts at the Old-Bailey. Now, unquestionably, at that august court,
when it is a question whether a culprit shall be spared, or whipped and
transported for life, probabilities should be sifted with a merciful leaning
towards the side of doubt. But the theatre is not the Old-Bailey, and as
we go to the former place for amusement, we open our hearts to whatever
may most amuse us ; nor do we thank the critic who, by his Old-Bailey-
like pleadings, would disenchant our belief. The imagination is a liberal
creditor of its faith as to incidents, when the poet can either touch our
affections, or tickle our ridicule.
    " Nay, we must not overlook an important truth in this subject. The
poet or the fictionist—and every great fictionist is a true poet—gives us
an image of life at large, and not of the narrow and stinted probabilities
of every-day life. But real life teems with events which, unless we knew
them to have actually happened, would seem to be next to impossibil-
ities. So that if you chain down the poet from representing every thing
that may seem in dry reasoning to be improbable, you will make his fiction cease to be a probable picture of Nature."
    8. *Steps me.* For the expletive *me*, see Gr. 220. Cf. 24 below, where
Rowe omits the word.
    Trencher. Wooden platter. K. remarks : " That the daughter of a
Duke of Milan should eat her capon from a trencher, may appear somewhat strange. It may be noted, however, that the fifth Earl of Northumberland, in 1512, was ordinarily served on wooden trenchers, and that
plates of pewter, mean as we may now think them, were reserved in his
family for great holidays. The Northumberland Household Book, edited
by Bishop Percy, furnishes several entries which establish this. In the
privy-purse expenses of Henry VIII. there are also entries regarding
trenchers ; as, for example, in 1530,—' Item, paied to the s'geant of the
pantrye for certen trenchors for the king, xxiijs. iiijd.' "
    9. *Keep himself.* Restrain himself.
    23. *Wot.* Know. Used only in the present tense and the participle *wot-
ting,* for which see *W. T.* p. 175.

25. *His servant.* Pope (followed by H.) changes *his* to "their ;" but, as Malone remarks, the words could never have been confounded either by the eye or ear. The inaccuracy is, moreover, in perfect keeping with the character.

47. *Offer her this.* The Coll. MS. adds "cur."

48. *The other squirrel.* Launce evidently compares the little dog to a squirrel ; but Hanmer reads "the other, Squirrel," as if *Squirrel* were the name of the pup.

49. *Hangman boys.* The 1st folio has "hangmans boyes," and the later folios "hangmans boy ;" but *hangman* was often used as a term of contempt, and Sr. is probably right in taking it so here. The Coll. MS. has "a hangman boy."

55. *Still an end.* Perpetually ; thought by Schmidt to be corrupted from "still and anon."

56. *Entertained.* Taken into service. See on ii. 4. 102 above.

66. *She lov'd me well deliver'd it to me.* For the ellipsis of the relative, see Gr. 244.

67. *To leave.* In parting with. For the infinitive, see on ii. 6. 1 above. Cf. 137 below.

86. *Poor fool!* "An expression used by S. more in the sense of compassionate tenderness than in that of describing folly ; though here there is also a spice of the latter indicated, as Julia thinks of her weakness in still loving Proteus" (Clarke). Cf. *A. Y. L.* p. 151.

100. *Speed.* Prosper, succeed. Cf. *W. T.* p. 161, note on *Sped.*

101. *Mean.* See on ii. 7. 5 above.

115. *Unadvis'd.* Inadvertently. Cf. *R. of L.* 1488: "And friend to friend gives unadvised wounds."

133. *Tender.* Have regard for. Cf. *Rich. III.* i. 1. 44 : "Tendering my person's safety ;" *Id.* ii. 4. 72 :

> "and so betide to me
> As well I tender you and all of yours!"

Ham. i. 3. 107 : "Tender yourself more dearly," etc.

146. *Sun-expelling mask.* In the poet's time ladies wore masks to protect their complexion. Cf. *T. and C.* i. 2. 286 : "my mask, to defend my beauty ;" *Cymb.* v. 3. 21 :

> "With faces fit for masks. or rather fairer
> Than those for preservation cas'd, or shame;"

W. T. iv. 4. 223 : "Masks for faces and for noses," etc. Silvia wears a mask when she is met in the forest (v. 2. 40 below).

148. *Lily-tincture.* The lily colour. Cf. *W. T.* iii. 2. 206 :

> "if you can bring
> Tincture or lustre in her lip, her eye," etc.

149. *That.* So that. Cf. ii. 1. 27 and iii. 1. 109 above.

152. *Pageants.* Dramatic exhibitions. Cf. *M. N. D.* p. 163, note on *Fond pageant.* See also on v. 4. 161 below.

153. *The woman's part.* All the female parts on the stage were played by boys or young men in the time of S. See *A. Y. L.* p. 201, note on *If I were a woman.*

158. *Agood.* In good earnest; used by S. only here. Malone quotes Marlowe, *Jew of Malta:* "I have laugh'd a-good;" and Turbervile, *Tragicall Tales:* "Whereat she waylde and wept a-good."

160. *Passioning.* Sorrowing; as in *V. and A.* 1059: "Dumbly she passions," etc. We find another allusion to the desertion of Ariadne by Theseus in *M. N. D.* ii. 1. 80.

166. *Beholding.* "Beholden," which Pope substituted, but which is not found in S. Gr. 372.

174. *Cold.* Cf. *M. of V.* ii. 7. 73 : "Fare you well ; your suit is cold," etc.

175. Coll. remarks here : "It has been objected by Sir T. Hanmer that after Silvia has gone out, and Julia is left alone, she still keeps up her character of servant to Proteus, and talks of her *master* and *mistress ;* but nothing could surely be more natural, and in the very next line S. makes Julia excuse it : 'Alas ! how love can trifle with itself !'"

178. *Tire.* Head-dress. Cf. *Much Ado,* p. 148.

181. *Flatter with.* Cf. *T. N.* i. 5. 322 : "to flatter with his lord," etc.

182. *Auburn.* Flaxen. Florio refers to "that whitish colour of women's hair which we call an Alburne or Aburne colour." The folios have "Aburne" here.

184. *Periwig.* False hair was much worn by women in the time of S. On his antipathy to the fashion, see *M. of V.* p. 149.

185. *Grey as glass.* The later folios have "grass" for *glass,* and the Coll. MS. "green as grass." On grey eyes in S. see *R. and J.* pp. 169, 172 ; and for green eyes, *Id.* p. 198.

186. *Mine's as high.* Pope reads "mine is high."

188. *Respective.* Worthy of being *respected,* or cared for. Elsewhere in S. the word is active in meaning (=caring for, regardful), as in *M. of V.* v. 1. 156: "You should have been respective and have kept it ;" *R. and J.* iii. 1. 128 : "Away to heaven, respective lenity !" etc. For *unrespective,* see *Rich. III.* p. 224. Cf. Gr. 3.

189. *Fond.* See on i. 1. 52 above.

194. *Statue.* Image, embodied shape. The word appears to have been sometimes used interchangeably with *picture,* but it is not necessary to explain it so here. Julia means, as she says, that Proteus might have her *substance* as a *statue* — a *substantial* image — in place of the mere *shadow,* or *superficial* image, in the painting. Hanmer reads "sainted," and Warb. "statued."

ACT V.

SCENE I.—3. *Friar.* Omitted by Steevens (ed. of 1793).
6. *Expedition.* Metrically five syllables. Gr. 476.

SCENE II.—7. *But love,* etc. The folios assign this to Proteus ; but, as Boswell conjectured, it belongs to Julia, to whom the recent editors generally give it.

10. *Black.* Of a dark complexion ; often opposed to *fair.* Cf. *Much Ado,* iii. 1. 63, *L. L. L.* iv. 3. 253, etc.

"A black man is a jewel in a fair woman's eye" is found in Ray's *Proverbs.*

13. *'T is true,* etc. The folios give this to Thurio ; corrected by Rowe.

14. *Wink.* Shut my eyes. See on i. 2. 139 above.

28. *Owe.* "Own" (Pope's reading) ; as often. Gr. 290.

29. *Out by lease.* That is, let to others, and not under his own control. Steevens quotes *Edin. Rev.* Nov. 1786 : "By Thurio's *possessions* he himself understands his lands and estate. But Proteus chooses to take the word likewise in a figurative sense, as signifying his *mental endowments ;* and when he says they are *out by lease,* he means that they are no longer enjoyed by their master (who is a fool), but are leased out to another."

32. *Sir Eglamour.* The 1st folio omits *Sir,* and the 2d and 3d folios have "say saw Sir."

41. *Confession.* A quadrisyllable. See on v. 1. 6 above.

49. *Peevish.* Silly, wayward. See on iii. 1. 68 above.

SCENE III.—4. *Learn'd.* Taught. See on ii. 6. 13 above.

8. *Moyses.* The folio reading, for which most eds. substitute Capell's "Moses." May it not have been intended for *Moise,* the Italian form of *Moses?*

11. *Scape.* Not to be printed "'scape," being found also in prose. Cf. Wb. s. v.

SCENE IV.—2. *These shadowy, desert,* etc. The folios have "This shadowy desart, unfrequented woods ;" corrected in the Coll. MS.

6. *Record.* Sing ; as in *Per.* iv. prol. 27 :

"She sung, and made the night-bird mute
That still records with moan."

Steevens cites, among other instances of the word in this sense, B. and F., *Pilgrim :* "O sweet, sweet ! how the birds record too !"

12. *Forlorn.* For the accent, see on i. 2. 124 above.

14. *'T is sure, my mates.* The folios have "These are my mates," and the Coll. MS. "These my rude mates." *'Tis sure* is due to Sr.

20. *Respect not.* Care not for. Cf. i. 2. 134 and iii. 1. 89 above. See also 54 below.

37. *Tender to me.* Dear to me ; perhaps the only instance of this passive sense of the word in S.

43. *Still approv'd.* Ever proved so by experience. Cf. *Lear,* ii. 2. 167 : "approve the common saw," etc. For *still*=ever, constantly, cf. *Ham.* ii. 2. 42 : "Thou still hast been the father of good news," etc. Gr. 69.

49. *To love me.* In loving me. See on ii. 6. 1 above. The later folios read "to deceive me."

55. *Spirit.* Often monosyllabic (=*sprite*). Gr. 463.

58. *And love you,* etc. The measure is not unlike that of many lines in S., but the critics cannot let it alone. H. reads "And love you 'gainst love's nature,—I will force ye." Walker says that "one of these *forces* [in 58 and 59] must be wrong ;" but neither he nor H. can "suggest a

remedy." To us the repetition seems perfectly natural, if the preceding line is left as S. doubtless wrote it.

67. *When one's own right hand.* The 1st folio omits *own*, which Johnson supplied. The later folios have "trusted now."

71. *Accurst.* Changed by Johnson to "curst." For *deep'st* (not contracted in the folios), see Gr. 473.

73. *Confounds.* Changed by some editors to "confound;" but see on iv. 3. 32 above. The Coll. MS. fills out the measure thus: "My shame and desperate guilt at once confound me." In 72 it has "'Mongst all my foes a friend," etc.

78. *Receive.* Acknowledge, believe; as in *Macb.* i. 7. 77: "Who dares receive it other?" etc.

83. *All that was mine,* etc. This is a startling piece of generosity, to say the least, and Blackstone proposed to get rid of it by transferring lines 82 and 83 to the end of Thurio's speech, 132-135 below. Hanmer considered the passage as "one great proof that the main parts of this play did not proceed from S." Malone and others ascribe the improbability to the poet's youth. Cf. pp. 19, 38 above. Clarke remarks: "This line—the overstrained generosity of which startles most sedate readers—is precisely in keeping with the previous speech, and with Valentine's character. He is a man of impulse, of warm, quick feelings, full of romance and enthusiasm; he is willing to make a heroic sacrifice to show his suddenly restored faith in his repentant friend, and works himself up to the requisite pitch of superhuman courage by the emulative reference to Divine mercy; but we see by his subsequent speech to Thurio how strongly his love for Silvia maintains itself within his bosom, though he fancies *for the moment* that he could make it ancillary to friendship. The generous ardour of Valentine's character is again visible in his appeal to the Duke on behalf of 'these banished men,' his companions; and the moral effect which his own virtuous principle, precept, and example have wrought upon them in their reform is of a piece with Shakespeare's noble philosophy of good in evil, thus early visible in this his certainly youthful production." W. says: "Valentine displays a similar overstrained generosity when, on the arrival of Proteus (ii. 4), he twice earnestly requests Silvia to receive his friend as her lover, on equal terms with him—as his 'fellow-servant' to her." See, however, on ii. 1. 90. It is to be noted that Silvia does not speak again in the play.

94. *Cry you mercy.* Beg your pardon. Cf. *M. N. D.* p. 159.

96. *Depart.* Cf. 2 *Hen. VI.* i. 1. 2: "At my depart for France," etc.

101. *Give aim to all thy oaths.* Was the object to which they were directed.

103. *Cleft the root.* That is, of her heart. The allusion to archery is kept up. Cf. *R. and J.* ii. 4. 15: "the very pin of his heart cleft with the blind bow-boy's butt-shaft;" the *pin* being the centre of the *clout,* or mark, at which the arrow was aimed. Hanmer reads "root on 't."

105. *Have took.* S. uses *took, taken,* and *ta'en* for the participle. Cf. *mistook* in 94 above.

106. *If shame live,* etc. "That is, if it be any shame to wear a disguise for the purposes of love" (Johnson).

117. *Close.* Union; as in *T. N.* v. i. 161: "Attested by the holy close of lips" (that is, a kiss), etc.

127. *The measure of my wrath.* "The length of my sword, the reach of my anger" (Johnson).

129. *Verona shall not hold thee.* However we may explain this (see on iii. 1. 81 above), it is probably what S. wrote. W. says: "To Valentine's apprehension, the whole party were on their way from Milan to Verona, as he was when the outlaws stayed him; and therefore his threat to Thurio that he shall never reach his destination." Theo. reads: "Milan shall not behold thee;" Hanmer: "And Milan shall not hold thee;" the Coll. MS.: "Milano shall not hold thee."

137. *Make such means.* Make such efforts, take such pains. Cf. *Rich. III.* v. 3. 40: "Sweet Blunt, make some good means to speak with him;" *Cymb.* ii. 4. 3: "What means do you make to him?" etc.

138. *Conditions.* A quadrisyllable. See on v. 1. 6 above.

141. *Worthy of an empress' love.* Cf. ii. 4. 74 above.

142. *Griefs.* Grievances. See 1 *Hen. IV.* p. 192.

143. *Repeal.* Recall. See on iii. 1. 234 above.

144. *Plead a new state,* etc. The Camb. editors, V., and W. follow the pointing of the folios, which makes *plead* in the same construction as *forget, cancel,* and *repeal.* We prefer, on the whole (with Steevens, K., Sr., St., D., Clarke, and H.), to take *Plead* as imperative. The Duke bids Valentine set up the plea of a new state on the score of his unrivalled merit, to which he himself will subscribe by allowing that he is a gentleman of good birth and therefore worthy of Silvia.

152. *Kept withal.* Kept company with, dwelt with. See *Ham.* p. 199.

160. *Include.* Hanmer reads "conclude," to which the word seems here to be equivalent. Schmidt gives it the same sense in *T. and C.* i. 3. 119: "Then every thing includes itself in power."

161. *With triumphs,* etc. "Malone, in a note on this passage, says: '*Triumphs,* in this and many other passages of Shakspere, signify masques and revels.' This assertion appears to us to have been hastily made. We have referred to all the passages of Shakspere in which the plural noun *triumphs* is used; and it appears to us to have a signification perfectly distinct from that of masques and revels. And first of *Julius Cæsar,* Antony says:

> 'O, mighty Cæsar! Dost thou lie so low?
> Are all thy conquests, glories, triumphs, spoils,
> Shrunk to this little measure?'

In *Titus Andronicus,* Tamora, addressing her conqueror, exclaims:

> 'We are brought to Rome
> To beautify thy triumphs.'

In these two quotations we have the original meaning of *triumphs*—namely, the solemn processions of a conqueror with his captives and spoils of victory. The triumphs of modern times were gorgeous shows, in imitation of those pomps of antiquity. When Columbus, returning from his first voyage, presented to the sovereigns of Castile and Arragon the productions of the countries which he had discovered, the solemn procession on that memorable occasion was a real *triumph.* But when

Edward IV., in Shakspere (*Henry VI., Part III.*), exclaims, after his final conquest,

> 'And now what rests, but that we spend the time
> With stately triumphs, mirthful comic shows,
> Such as befit the pleasures of the court,'

he refers to those ceremonials which the genius of chivalry had adopted from the mightier pomps of antiquity, imitating something of their splendour, but laying aside their stern demonstrations of outward exultation over their vanquished foes. There were no human captives in massive chains—no lions and elephants led along to the amphitheatre, for the gratification of a turbulent populace. Edward exclaims of his prisoner Margaret:

> 'Away with her, and waft her hence to France.'

The dread of Cleopatra was that of exposure in the triumph:

> 'Shall they hoist me up,
> And show me to the shouting varletry
> Of censuring Rome?'

Here, then, was the difference of the Roman and the feudal manners. The triumphs of the Middle Ages were shows of peace, decorated with the pomp of arms; but altogether mere scenic representations, deriving their name from the more solemn triumphs of antiquity. But they were not masques, as Malone has stated. The Duke of York, in *Richard II.*, asks:

> 'What news from Oxford? hold these justs and triumphs?'

and for these 'justs and triumphs' Aumerle has prepared his 'gay apparel.' There is one more passage which appears to us conclusive as to the use of the word *triumphs*. The passage is in *Pericles*: Simonides asks:

> 'Are the knights ready to begin the triumph?'

And when answered that they are, he says:

> 'Return then, we are ready; and our daughter,
> In honour of whose birth these triumphs are,
> Sits here, like beauty's child.'

The triumph, then, meant the 'joustes of peace' which we have noticed in a previous illustration [see on i. 3. 30 above]; and the great tournament there mentioned, when Elizabeth sat in her 'fortress of perfect beauty,' was expressly called a triumph. In the triumph were, of course, included the processions and other 'stately' shows that accompanied the sports of the tilt-yard. . . .

"'The Duke of Milan, in this play, desires to 'include all jars,' not only with 'triumphs,' but with 'mirth and rare solemnity.' The 'mirth' and the 'solemnity' would include the 'pageant'—the favourite show of the days of Elizabeth. The 'masque' (in its highest signification) was a more refined and elaborate device than the pageant; and, therefore, we shall confine the remainder of this illustration to some few general observations on the subject of 'pageants.'

"We may infer, from the expression of Julia in the fourth act,

> 'At Pentecost,
> When all our pageants of delight were play'd,'

that the pageant was a religious ceremonial, connected with the festivals of the church. And so it originally was. The 'pageants' performed at Coventry were, for the most part, 'dramatic mysteries ;' and the city, according to Dugdale, was famous, before the suppression of the monasteries, for the pageants that were played there on Corpus Christi day. 'These pageants,' says the fine old topographer, 'were acted with mighty state and reverence by the fryers of this house, and contained the story of the New Testament, which was composed into old English rhyme. The theatres for the several scenes were very large and high, and being placed upon wheels, were drawn to all the eminent places of the city, for the better advantage of the spectators.' It appears, from Mr. Sharp's *Dissertation on the Coventry Pageants,* that the trading companies were accustomed to perform these plays ; and it will be remembered that when Elizabeth was entertained by Leicester at Kenilworth, the 'old Coventry play of *Hock Tuesday*' formed a principal feature of the amusements. The play of *Hock Tuesday* commemorates the great victory over the Danes, A.D. 1002, and it was exhibited before the queen by Captain Cox and many others from Coventry. The Whitsun plays at Chester, called the Chester Pageants, or Chester Mysteries, were also performed by the trading companies of that ancient city. Archdeacon Rogers, who died in 1569, has left an account of the Whitsun plays, which he saw in Chester, which shows that the pageant-vehicles there, like those of Coventry, were scaffolds upon wheels. Mr. Collier, in his valuable *History of the Stage,* mentions a fact, given by Hall the historian, that in 1511, at the revels at Whitehall, Henry VIII. and his lords 'entered the hall in a pageant on wheels.'

" It is clear from the passage in which Julia describes her own part in the 'pageants of delight,'—

> 'Ariadne passioning
> For Theseus' perjury and unjust flight,'—→

that the pageant had begun to assume something of the classical character of the masque. But it had certainly not become the gorgeous entertainment which Johnson has so glowingly described, as 'of power to surprise with delight, and steal away the spectators from themselves.' The pageant in which Julia acted at Pentecost was probably such as Shakspere had seen in the streets of Coventry, or in some stately baronial hall of his rich county " (K.).

169. *That.* So that. See on ii. 1. 27 above.

Fortuned. Happened. In *A. and C.* i. 2. 77, it means to tell or fix the fortune of. S. uses the verb but twice.

171. *Loves discovered.* Pope reads "love" for *loves,* and the Coll. MS. "love's discoverer."

172. *That done.* Omitted in the Coll. MS., which adds "no less" at the end of the line.

ADDENDUM.

THE "TIME-ANALYSIS" OF THE PLAY.—We give below the summing-up of Mr. P. A. Daniel's "time-analysis" in his elaborate paper " On

the Times or Durations of the Action of Shakspere's Plays " (*Trans. of New Shakspere Soc.* 1877-79, p. 123), with some explanatory extracts from the preceding pages appended as foot-notes:
   "The time of this play comprises seven days, represented on the stage, and intervals.
   "Day 1. Act. I. sc. i. and ii.
         Interval: a month, perhaps ; perhaps sixteen months.*
   "   2. Act I. sc. iii. and Act II. sc. i.†
   "   3. Act II. sc. ii. and iii.
         Interval: Proteus's journey to Milan.
   "   4. Act II. sc. iv. and v.
         Interval of a few days, to allow Proteus to settle at court.
   "   5. Act II. sc. vi. and vii., Act III., and Act IV. sc. i.
         Interval, including Julia's journey to Milan.
   "   6. Act IV. sc. ii.‡
   "   7. Act IV. sc. iii. and iv., and Act V." §

---

* " Time to hear of Valentine's arrival at Milan and of his success at court ; time for Julia to acknowledge her love to Proteus. For a month past Antonio has been hammering on the question of sending Proteus abroad. We may perhaps allow a month for this interval. In Act IV sc. i., however, Valentine, interrogated by the outlaws, says that he has sojourned in Milan ' some sixteen months ;' and he also says that he was banished for killing a man. Some motive for the self-accusation of murder may be conceived : it would impress the outlaws with the belief that he was a man of desperate fortunes, and therefore fit for their purpose ; but why he should deceive them as to the time of his sojourn in Milan is not so clear. The *sixteen months* is not wanted for the plot of the play ; but if accepted, its place must be in the first ' interval.'
   † " I place this scene in day No. 2. though it might equally well come in the following day It must from its position be coincident in point of time either with Act I. sc. iii. or with Act II. sc. ii. and iii.
   ‡ " At night. Thurio serenades Silvia. This fact would at first sight seem to connect the scene with day No. 5. and lead us to suppose that Thurio was now putting in practice his resolution of Act III. sc. ii. There are, however, so many separating incidents in the scene, that one is fairly driven to the conclusion that this serenade is one of a later date than that resolved on in Act III. sc. ii. In the first place we find Proteus, at the beginning of the scene, speaking as though he had been for some time—days at least— urging his suit to Silvia, since, by the Duke's permission, he had obtained access to her. He tells her, too, he has heard that Valentine is dead ; it is a lie, of course, but one he could not have ventured on if this were only the night of the day on which Valentine was banished : it implies a lapse of time His courtship of Silvia has, in fact, become notorious, and mine host brings Julia (as Sebastian)—who has apparently arrived in Milan within the last few hours—to this serenade under Silvia's window, as to a place to which it is well known Proteus often resorts. The presence of Julia, too, whose resolution to follow Proteus is only made known in Act II. sc. vii. (day No. 5), would be a glaring impossibility if this scene were taken to be the night of that same day. Time for her journey must be allowed, and an interval supposed between this scene and those preceding it
   § " It may perhaps be questioned whether the two last scenes should not be placed in a separate day ; but taking into consideration the extreme rapidity of the action of the play generally, it seems probable that they were intended to end the day commencing with Act IV. sc. iii."

INDEX OF WORDS AND PHRASES EXPLAINED.

---

account of, 130.
adventure (=venture), 139.
advice, more, 135.
advice, upon, 139.
agone, 139.
agood, 150.
aim (=guess), 138.
ale (=church-ale), 136.
allicholly, 146.
and there an end, 131.
angerly, 125.
apparent (=manifest), 139.
applaud (=approve), 129.
approved (=proved), 151.
as (omitted), 146.
as (=that), 133.
auburn, 150.
awful (=full of awe), 145.

bare (play upon), 141.
be moved, 132.
beadsman, 122.
beauty lives with kindness, 146.
bechance, 123.
befortune, 147.
beholding (=beholden), 150.
belike, 130.
beshrew me, 124, 133.
best, you were, 123, 127.
bestow myself, 139.
bid the base, 125.
black (=dark), 150.
blunt (=stupid), 136.
boots, give me not the, 123.
bosom, in thy, 140.
bottom (=wind), 143.
break with him, 129, 138.
broken (=fallen out), 135.
broker (=go-between), 124.
buried (trisyllable), 146.
but one knave, 140.
by (=of), 134.
by my halidom, 146.

canker (=worm), 123.
cate-log, 141.
censure (=judge), 124.
chameleon (feeding on air), 132.

charactered (accent), 136.
circumstance, 123, 142.
cite (=urge), 133.
cleft the root, 152.
clerkly (adverb), 131.
close (=union), 153.
coat (play upon), 132.
codpiece, 138.
coil (=ado), 125.
culd, 150.
competitor (=partner), 136.
conceit (=opinion), 142.
conceitless, 146.
conditions (metre), 153.
confession (metre), 151.
conjure (accent), 136.
consort, 143, 145.
contents (=pleases), 139.
conversed (=associated), 133.
cover of the salt, 142.
crews, 145.
cry you mercy, 152.
curst, 142.

dazzled (trisyllable), 129, 135.
deep'st, 152.
depart (noun), 152.
descant, 125.
destined to a drier death, 124.
dispose (noun), 138, 145.
Don, 132.
doublet, 132.
dump, 144.

earnest (play upon), 131.
enforce (=force), 147.
engine, 140.
entertain (=employ), 133, 149.
exhibition (=allowance), 129.
exile (accent), 142.
expedition (metre), 150.
extreme (accent), 137.

farthingale, 138.
fearful-hanging, 125.
feature (=form), 133.
figure, 131.
fire (dissyllable), 124, 137.
flatter with, 150.

fond (=doting), 123, 150.
for (=because), 134, 140, 147.
for (=for fear of), 126.
for why, 139.
forlorn (accent), 125, 151.
fortuned, 155.

gave aim to, 152.
give me not the boots, 123.
give us leave, 138.
give ye good even, 130.
gossips (play upon), 140.
greed (=agreed), 134.
grey as glass, 150.
griefs (=grievances), 153.
grievance (=grief), 144.
grievances, 147.

halidom, 146.
Hallowmas, 130.
hangman boys, 149.
have you the tongues? 144.
his (=its), 142.
home-keeping youth, etc, 122.
hour's (dissyllable), 142.
how sayest thou? 135.
however (=in any case), 123.

impeachment, 127.
importunacy (accent), 146.
importune (accent), 127, 140.
impose (noun), 147.
impress (accent), 142.
in good time, 129.
in print, 131.
include (=conclude), 153.
infinite of love, 138.
inherit (=win), 144.
inly (adjective), 137.
inquire you forth, 134.
interpret (of puppets), 130.
it shall go hard, 123.

jade (play upon), 141.
jerkin, 132.
jolt-head, 141.

keep himself, 148.
kept withal, 153.
kind (=kindred), 132.

laced mutton, 123.
Leander, 122.
learn (=teach), 136, 151.
leave (=leave off), 136, 140.
lets (=hinders), 139.
liberal (=too free), 142.
lie (play upon), 125.
lies (=lodges), 146.
Light o' love, 125.
likes (=pleases), 146.
lily-tincture, 149.
lime (=bird-lime), 143.
longing, 138.

make such means, 153.
manage (=handle), 140.
mean (=means), 136, 138, 149.
mean (=tenor), 125.
measure of my wrath, 153.
Merops, 140.
moist (verb), 143.
month's mind, a, 126.
mood (=rage), 145.
more advice, 135.
more hair than wit, 142.
most heaviest, 147.
motion(=puppet-show), 130.
Moyses, 151.
muse (=wonder), 129.

noddy (play upon), 124.
noise (=musicians), 144.

ocean (trisyllable), 137.
o'erlooked (=perused), 124.
omitting (=neglecting), 133.
on (=of), 146.
on (play upon), 129.
one (play upon), 129.
onset, 144.
out by lease, 151.
out of all nick, 146.
owe (=own), 151.

pageants, 149.
Panthion, 122.
pardon you, 144.
parle, 124.
parting (=departure), 132.
passenger, 144.
passioning, 150.
peevish (=foolish), 139, 151.
periwig, 150.
persevers, 142.
Phaethon, 140.
picture (figurative), 135.
pin (of target), 152.
pinfold, 124.
plead a new state, etc., 153.
poor fool, 147.
practising (=plotting), 145.

praise her liquor, 142.
pretence (=intention), 138.
pretend (=intend , 136.
principality, 134.
proper (=comely), 144.
protestation (metre), 125.
Protheus, 122.
publisher, 138.
puling, 130.

quaintly, 131, 139.
quality (=profession), 145.
quips, 145.
quote (=note), 132.

reasoning (=talking), 131.
receive (=believe , 152.
recking (=caring), 147.
record (=sing), 151.
remorseful, 147.
repeal (=recall), 140. 153.
reputation (metre), 138.
resembleth (quadrisyllable), 129.
respect (=care about), 126, 139, 151.
respective, 150.
rhyme and reason, 131.
road (=port), 123, 134.
Robin Hood's fat friar, 144.

sad (=serious), 126.
Saint Gregory's well, 146.
Saint Nicholas be thy speed! 141.
scape, 151.
servant, 130.
set (play upon), 130.
set (=set to music), 125.
set the world on wheels, 141.
several (=separate), 125.
she (=her), 130.
sheep (play upon), 123.
ship (play upon), 123.
shot (play upon), 135.
silly (=poor, harmless), 145.
sith, 126.
slender reputation, 126.
so (=so be it), 131.
so ho, so ho! 140.
sort (=select), 144.
speed (=prosper), 149.
spirit (monosyllable), 151.
squirrel, 149.
statue, 150.
stead (verb), 131.
still an end, 149.
still (=ever), 151.
stock (=stocking), 141.
stomach (play upon), 125.
sudden quips, 145.
suggest (=tempt), 136, 138.

summer-swelling, 134.
sun-bright, 139.
sun-expelling mask, 149.
sweet mouth, 142.
sweet-suggesting, 136.
swinged, 130, 142.

table (=tablet), 136.
takes diet, 130.
tarriance, 138.
tender (=dear), 151.
tender (=have regard for), 149.
testerned, 124.
that (=so that), 130, 139, 142. 149, 155.
throughly, 125.
timeless, 138.
tire (=head-dress), 150.
to (=for), 139.
to (= in comparison with), 133.
to (omitted), 147.
too too, 135.
took (=taken), 152.
touch, 137.
trenched (=cut), 142.
trencher, 148.
triumphs, 153.
true devoted pilgrim, 136.
turn (=be inconstant), 132.

unadvised, 149.
understands (play upon), 135.
ungartered, 130.
up and down, 132.
upon advice, 139.

Valentinus, 129.
very (adjective), 143.

waxen image, 135.
weeds (=garments), 138.
were I best, 127.
what (=what a), 125.
where (=whereas), 139.
who (=whom), 140.
wink (=shut the eyes), 126, 133, 151.
with (=by), 130.
with circumstance, 142.
withal, 153.
without (play upon), 130.
woman's part, 149.
wood (=mad), 132.
world on wheels, the, 141.
worthies, 134.
wot, 148.
wrack, 124.
wreathe your arms, 130.

you were best, 123.

SHAKESPEARE.

WITH NOTES BY WM. J. ROLFE, Litt.D.

The Merchant of Venice.
The Tempest.
Julius Cæsar.
Hamlet.
As You Like It.
Henry the Fifth.
Macbeth.
Henry the Eighth.
A Midsummer-Night's Dream.
Richard the Second.
Richard the Third.
Much Ado About Nothing.
Antony and Cleopatra.
Romeo and Juliet.
Othello.
Twelfth Night.
The Winter's Tale.
King John.
Henry IV. Part I.
Henry IV. Part II.

King Lear.
The Taming of the Shrew.
All's Well That Ends Well.
Coriolanus.
Comedy of Errors.
Cymbeline.
Merry Wives of Windsor.
Measure for Measure.
Two Gentlemen of Verona.
Love's Labor 's Lost.
Timon of Athens.
Henry VI. Part I.
Henry VI. Part II.
Henry VI. Part III.
Troilus and Cressida.
Pericles, Prince of Tyre.
The Two Noble Kinsmen.
Poems.
Sonnets.
Titus Andronicus.

Illustrated. 16mo, Cloth, 56 cents per vol.; Paper, 40 cents per vol.
FRIENDLY EDITION, complete in 20 vols., 16mo, Cloth, $30 00 ; Half Calf, $60 00. (*Sold only in Sets.*)

In the preparation of this edition of the English Classics it has been the aim to adapt them for school and home reading, in essentially the same way as Greek and Latin Classics are edited for educational purposes. The chief requisites are a pure text (expurgated, if necessary), and the notes needed for its thorough explanation and illustration.

Each of Shakespeare's plays is complete in one volume, and is preceded by an Introduction containing the "History of the Play," the "Sources of the Plot," and "Critical Comments on the Play."

From HORACE HOWARD FURNESS, Ph.D., LL.D., *Editor of the "New Variorum Shakespeare."*

No one can examine these volumes and fail to be impressed with the conscientious accuracy and scholarly completeness with which they are edited. The educational purposes for which the notes are written Mr. Rolfe never loses sight of, but like "a well-experienced archer hits the mark his eye doth level at."

From F. J. FURNIVALL, *Director of the New Shakspere Society, London.*

The merit I see in Mr. Rolfe's school editions of Shakspere's Plays over those most widely used in England is that Mr. Rolfe edits the plays as works of a poet, and not only as productions in Tudor English. Some editors think that all they have to do with a play is to state its source and explain its hard words and allusions ; they treat it as they would a charter or a catalogue of household furniture, and then rest satisfied. But Mr. Rolfe, while clearing up all verbal difficulties as carefully as any Drynsdust, always adds the choicest extracts he can find, on the spirit and special " note " of each play, and on the leading characteristics of its chief personages. He does *not* leave the student without help in getting at Shakspere's chief attributes, his characterization and poetic power. And every practical teacher knows that while every boy can look out hard words in a lexicon for himself, not one in a score can, unhelped, catch points of and realize character, and feel and express the distinctive individuality of each play as a poetic creation.

From Prof. EDWARD DOWDEN, LL.D., *of the University of Dublin, Author of "Shakspere : His Mind and Art."*

I incline to think that no edition is likely to be so useful for school and home reading as yours. Your notes contain so much accurate instruction, with so little that is superfluous ; you do not neglect the æsthetic study of the plays; and in externals, paper, type, binding, etc., you make a book " pleasant to the eye " (as well as " to be desired to make one wise ")—no small matter, I think, with young readers and with old.

From EDWIN A. ABBOTT, M.A., *Author of "Shakespearian Grammar."*

I have not seen any edition that compresses so much necessary information into so small a space, nor any that so completely avoids the common faults of commentaries on Shakespeare—needless repetition, superfluous explanation, and unscholar-like ignoring of difficulties.

From HIRAM CORSON, M.A., *Professor of Anglo-Saxon and English Literature, Cornell University, Ithaca, N. Y.*

In the way of annotated editions of separate plays of Shakespeare for educational purposes, I know of none quite up to Rolfe's.